FORT DESPAIR

Other books by this author available
from New English Library:

FORT DESPAIR
George G. Gilman

NEW ENGLISH LIBRARY/TIMES MIRROR

A New English Library Original Publication, 1979

© 1979 by George G. Gilman

First NEL paperback edition November 1979

NEL Books are published by
New English Library Limited from
Barnard's Inn, Holborn,
London EC1N 2JR.
Made and printed in Great Britain by
Hunt Barnard Printing Ltd.,
Aylesbury, Bucks.

45004379 **7**

For:

Liz – faithful companion
to another new rider of
the blood-stained sage!

Chapter One

Adam Steele felt the rush of displaced air cross the left side of his face. Heard the crack of the rifle shot and the thud and whine of the bullet as it impacted with a rock and ricocheted ten feet behind him. He had fisted a gloved hand around the frame of his booted Colt Hartford by then. And had shifted his gaze high and to the left: saw the tell-tale puff of white muzzle smoke against grey rock. Thus had the sharp-shooter's position precisely pinpointed before he reined his black stallion to a halt, slid his booted feet free of the stirrups and powered clear of the saddle.

The horse stood as if rooted to the hard-packed, dust-coated floor of the canyon by all four hooves. As Steele whirled and lunged for the cover of the rock off which the bullet had glanced. Despite the thud of his footfalls he heard the metallic sounds of a repeating rifle's action being pumped. And gritted his teeth as he curled himself into a ball the moment he hit the ground. Not entirely certain that the rock gave him complete protection from the highly placed rifleman.

The second report cracked and the bullet was another ricochet. Off the top of the rock this time. It sprayed splinters of rock against the back of Steele's neck before it spun to the right to impact with the cliff face which formed the hundred-foot-high north wall of the canyon.

Steele pushed out his legs, straightened his back and rolled on to his belly. There was no need to thumb back the hammer of the revolving rifle: that had been done as part of the same reflex action as he slid the Colt Hartford from the boot. The weapon was now gripped two-handed, a finger curled around the trigger, as he levered himself with his elbows towards the point where the rock was highest.

Another bullet was jacked into the breech of the repeater: and an instant later the sharp-shooter triggered it down into the canyon. It tunnelled a hole into the ground where, a part of a second before, Steele's left leg had been exposed.

Steele was squatting hard on his haunches by then, head bent so that his chin was pressed to his chest, his left shoulder and thigh leaning against the sun-warmed rock.

He half rose and half turned, threw the stock of the Colt Hartford to his shoulder and aligned his eye behind the rifle sights to draw a bead on the spot where he had seen the puff of muzzle smoke.

The topography of the canyon in which he was pinned down was firmly imprinted on his mind. For it was in the nature of Adam Steele to pay close attention to his surroundings at all times. To be constantly on his guard against a sudden attack such as this. But in an area like the Dakotas Badlands it needed more than one pair of careful eyes to watch every pocket of cover within gunshot range.

Steele had been aware of this all morning and for the first two hours of afternoon as he rode slowly across the spectacularly eroded terrain. Between high peaks, around towering rock pillars and along steep sided gullies. His route dictated by the formation of the landscape, but stage by stage picking his way in his chosen direction of south west.

It was a very hot day and so his pace was set as much by the need to conserve his own strength and that of his mount as by the hostile land he crossed. But he sweated nonetheless, and dust rose from beneath the slow-moving hooves of the stallion to billow and lodge in his clothing or adhere to the tacky surface of his skin.

And this had the effect of colouring him into the landscape – for at the start of the day's ride, freshly washed up and shaved and with his clothing hand-brushed, he had looked totally out of his element. Because Adam Steele was a former Virginian gentleman who at every opportunity sought to maintain certain of his one-time standards: primarily of cleanliness and mode of dress.

He was not a big man – he stood no more than a half inch taller than five feet six inches and had a build that was compact yet strong. Though the suggestion of physical power in his frame was not visible to the casual observer, seeming somehow to be camouflaged by his choice of clothing. For he dressed like a city dude. His suit, the jacket of which was now lashed to the bedroll behind the saddle on the stallion, was pale blue. His vest, which was unbuttoned to reveal the lace trim of his white shirt, was purple. He wore black riding boots and a low-crowned, wide-brimmed Stetson which was also black. Because of the blistering heat of the day he had taken off his string necktie and a grey silk kerchief was loosely knotted at the base of his throat. On his hands was a pair of black, skin-tight buckskin gloves.

The face between the hat and the kerchief was, at first glance, a match for the clothing in more than the mere fact that it showed many signs of long and hard wear. For, in total, the features had a brand of nondescript handsomeness which, to those who lacked perception, was occasionally – in combination with the dudish style of dress – mistaken for the surface sign of weakness of character.

It was a long, lean face with regular features, the eyes coal-black and the mouthline gentle. When he smiled there was an almost boyish quality in the expression. But in repose his eyes were cold and world-weary and his prematurely grey hair – showing hardly any trace of its former red colouration – which he wore neatly trimmed but allowed to grow long in sideburns, served to make him appear much older than his less than forty years. Now, as he took aim at a blue-clad shoulder just visible beside a rock on a shelf in the canyon wall, there was no expression at all on his weather-stained and time-lined face. Even though he had every intention of killing the man who had taken three shots at him.

The edge on which the sharpshooter was perched was cut into the cliff face where the canyon swung to the south to

9

close with the far wall and form a narrow exit from the towering escarpments which had been flanking Steele since mid-morning.

The south wall would have provided shade during the ride, but the Virginian had elected to forsake the coolness of this. To stay close to the base of the north cliff which had crumbled over the centuries to litter the ground beneath with the kind of covering rock he now leaned against. For elsewhere the canyon floor was a dangerously open area of dust-covered, hard-packed earth with just an occasional patch of tough scrub grass clinging tenaciously to life.

'Soldier!'

The single word was bellowed, in the tone of a man familiar with authority. And reached Steele's ears an instant after he had squeezed the trigger and heard the sharp crack of the Colt Hartford's report.

The bullet found its mark – the slender curve of blue against grey, 150 feet ahead and twenty feet up from the floor of the canyon. Steele saw the wound made, then a splash of dark crimson which was ejected from the exit hole to hit and run down the rock in back of the man on the ledge.

'Sonofabitch!' the injured man shrieked. As the impact of the bullet raised him to his full height and flung him back against the cliff face. Which in turn jarred the rifle from his hands. And the pain and rage which had spread across his bristled sweat-run features were displaced by deeply etched fear as he watched the repeater bounce on the edge of the ledge, teeter there for perhaps a full second, then topple over and drop to the ground.

Steele had unfolded to his full height by then, the Colt Hartford cocked again and held rock steady in his gloved hands: sights aligned on the chest of the man dressed in the blue uniform pants and shirt of an army trooper.

The trooper was transfixed by terror against the rock face. And moved only his eyes, shifting them from the point on the ledge where his rifle had tumbled from sight to stare down at Steele. The bloodstain high on his left shoulder expanded, to merge with the sweat mark at his armpit.

'Be much obliged if you don't kill him, sir!'

The wounded trooper had no gunbelt slung around his waist nor a handgun jutting from the waistband of his pants. But the Virginian continued to keep his rifle aimed as he shifted his impassive gaze to where a second uniformed figure was visible: seated astride a horse on the south rim of the canyon, at the point where the cliff faces came within twenty feet of touching. This man was a cavalry lieutenant, in full uniform. In the same thirtyish age group as the trooper. Travel-stained but far less dishevelled than the wounded man.

Steele confined his response to dropping one hand away from the rifle and twisting the wrist of the other to cant the barrel to his right shoulder. Then eased the hammer forward.

The man on the ledge sagged against the rock but did not crumple.

The lieutenant still had both hands cupped around his mouth in the form of a bullhorn. He yelled: 'Now be obliged to you again if you hold that soldier down there until I reach you!'

He did not wait for a response: quickly took up his reins and heeled his horse into a gallop. Out of sight beyond the canyon rim, heading west.

Steele moved around the rock and over to where the stallion still stood, having been unconcerned by the crash of gunfire.

During the time it took the Virginian to mount, slide the rifle into the boot, and urge his horse into movement, the sole action of the man on the ledge was to run his right hand over the wound in his left shoulder and grimace at the slick, wet crimson which coated his fingers. Then he fixed his resentful eyes on the slow-riding Steele.

He was six feet tall and extremely thin with a narrow, angular face: deep-set dark eyes, hollow cheeks, beaklike nose and prominent Adam's apple. With black hair cropped to within a quarter of an inch of his skull all over. There was a three day growth of bristles on his lower face, dark circles under his eyes and his skin was blotched red and scaled white by long exposure to a blistering sun. The tongue which came painfully out to touch his cracked lips was dry and swollen.

Steele halted his mount twenty feet out from the base of the cliff, immediately in front of the ledge. From where he could see the head and shoulders of the trooper: and also the series of naturally carved niches which the man had used to climb to his vantage point. An hour ago, perhaps, when he had glimpsed a lone rider emerging from the shimmering heat haze which hung like a curtain of damp mist in the distant east.

'Best you come down from there, trooper,' Steele drawled, the accent of his native Virginia still pronounced. 'You lose much more blood, you maybe won't make it.'

'Maybe I don't wanna make it,' the man answered, his voice croaky from thirst.

Steele lifted his shoulders no more than an inch and un-hooked one of the two canteens from his saddlehorn. 'No skin off the back of my throat, trooper.'

He took the stopper from the neck and raised the canteen to his lips.

'You lousy sonofabitch!' the man on the ledge rasped between his discoloured teeth. Then came away from the rock wall, groaning as movement caused a stab of pain to sear across his wounded shoulder.

Steele took only a short drink of the warm, tasteless water and then held the canteen against his thigh, stopper dangling, as he watched the lanky trooper climb slowly and painfully down from the ledge. The descent took all of five sweating, groaning, cursing minutes: the man hampered by the fact that his left arm hung uselessly at his side. He chose to drop the final six feet, hit the ground awkwardly, fell to the side and vented a shrill cry of agony as he sprawled out on to his back.

He lay like that, breathing as if each intake of air would be his last, until Steele and the stallion came close enough to cast their shadows across him. Then, eyes closed and teeth gritted against pain, he fought to sit up and turn so that his back rested against the base of the cliff.

'I guess now I made it down you ain't gonna give me a drink of water, mister?' he rasped, squinting up at the mounted man.

The Virginian reached the canteen down to him and he grasped it eagerly. But did not have the strength to snatch it from the tight grip of the gloved hand.

'Sonofa —' he started.

'Just a little for now,' Steele told him. 'You gulp it down it'll come back up again so fast you'll —'

'I know that! Man who's served two and a half stinkin' years in Godforsaken places like this —'

Steele had released his grip on the canteen and the trooper curtailed talk to suck water into his mouth. Just a little, which he swilled around with his tongue before he allowed it to trickle down his throat. He came close to spreading a smile across his emaciated features as he relished the effect of moisture soothing parched membranes. Then he asked:

'Don't guess you got anythin' stronger than water, mister?'

'You're right.'

'How about somethin' to smoke?'

A shake of the head. 'Just not your day, is it?'

The trooper took another drink, the same way as before. And gazed along the canyon towards the east. 'I'm sorry for what I done, mister,' he said with genuine regret. 'Blastin' off at you the way I did.'

'No harm done to me.'

The deep-set eyes shifted in their sockets and shortened focus to look up at the Virginian. 'But I was real desperate, mister.'

Steele nodded. 'Yeah.'

'See, it's not just water I was short on. I ain't eaten anythin' either, for four days. And I needed a horse, too. Some matches to light fires. Warm clothes and blankets for the nights. And ammo. There was only six shells left in my Winchester when I opened up at you. Why I wanted everythin' you got. Reason it was no use me tryin' to panhandle a swallow of water and a bite of grub off you.'

Steele nodded again. 'Man who's served more than two years in country like this should know better than to set out —'

The trooper tried to spit, but he did not have enough moisture in him yet. 'A liquored-up man don't think straight like a sober one, mister!' he snarled. 'The night I took off from Benedict I had two pints of rotgut swillin' around in my belly. And it seemed to me like I could walk clear home to Johnsbury Vermont.' His ire evaporated. He took another drink,

13

swallowed most of the water but spat out the rest. 'By the time the hangover got started I was too far away from the fort to turn back.' He shifted his gaze to peer along the canyon again. 'Should've, though. Been hung by now and hell can't be no worse than four days in the Badlands without food or water. What Major Friggin' McCoy does to deserters, mister. Hangs 'em.'

He squinted up at Steele and there was a tacit inquiry in his expression. But there was hopelessness, too. Replaced by resignation rather than resentment when the Virginian said:

'What did you ever do for me, trooper?'

The injured man, the blood on his shirt now black and crusted, held the canteen between his knees so that he could push in the stopper one handed. Then he held it out for Steele to take. As the sound of hooves hitting the ground at a canter came from between the sheer rock faces at the exit of the canyon.

'Here, mister. You give me more than I deserve. Army's problem now. To keep me alive until Major Friggin' McCoy gets a chance to hang me.'

Steele looped the strap of the canteen back over his saddle-horn. And glanced to the left as the lieutenant rode out into the canyon, reining his mount down to a walk and angling the animal across to where the Virginian and the trooper waited. As he halted his mount, the officer threw up a smart salute.

'Lieutenant Colvard, sir. Ninth Cavalry. Posted to Fort Benedict. I witnessed the unprovoked attack on you and you may rest assured this soldier will be brought to book for what he did.'

Colvard looked to be about thirty-one or two. An inch less than six feet tall. Black haired and green eyed. With a square-shaped, rugged-looking face, evenly tanned and unlined. His uniform looked relatively new under its covering of trail dust. He sat on his horse like one born to the saddle and well trained by the army.

'A man can only get hung once, lieutenant,' the trooper growled.

'Speak when you're spoken to, soldier!' Colvard snapped

and his expression became contemptuous as he looked down at the wounded man. 'What's your name?'

'Moody.'

'Sir! I'm an officer!'

'Same kind as Major Friggin' McCoy!' Moody rasped through teeth shown in a sneer. 'Makes you shit far as I'm concerned. And I don't call shit nothin' but what it is!'

Colvard suffered genuine shock at the response. To an extent where it constricted his throat for several seconds. But then he brought himself under control and glowered with deep hatred at Moody.

'On your feet, soldier,' he ordered, his tone of voice subdued but brittle. 'And if you do hang for whatever you've done, know this. You'll go to the gallows with one lash across your back for every time you bad mouth me between here and Fort Benedict.'

Moody used his good arm to help lever himself up from the ground, then his feet and back to reach his full height against the rock face. Beads of fresh sweat stood out on his filthy face and new blood broke through the crusting over his wound.

'And you're a shit as well, mister!' the trooper accused through clenched teeth as he moved away from the cliff. 'For not puttin' that bullet through my heart instead of my friggin' shoulder!'

The exhausting effects of four days on the move under a harsh sun without food or water, compounded by the shock of the bullet wound and the loss of blood, abruptly caused the man's faltering steps to drain his final reserve of strength. And he dropped hard to his knees, groaned, closed his eyes and pitched forward. To measure his unconscious length between the two mounted men.

Colvard looked relieved. 'Was wondering how to get the prisoner from here to the fort. He appears to have decided that for himself.'

'Reckon so,' the Virginian drawled as the officer swung down from the saddle. 'But according to how he sees it, he fell between two stools.'

15

Chapter Two

It took them the rest of the afternoon and all the following day from dawn to dusk to reach Fort Benedict, which was sited on the south western fringe of the Badlands. Lieutenant Colvard took full responsibility for the welfare and security of Moody which meant that while they were on the move the officer walked, leading his bay gelding by the reins.

For the first hour, the unconscious trooper was slumped across the saddle, arms and legs swinging in time with the clop of the slow moving horse. Then, when he came round, he sat drunkenly astride the gelding, feet in the stirrups and right hand gripping the saddlehorn. With one of Colvard's blankets draped over his head and shoulders: which caused him to quickly sweat out the little moisture he had drawn from Steele's canteen, but kept the harsh glare of the sun from further burning his flesh.

At night camp, the officer shared his food and water with the trooper and cleaned and dressed the shoulder wound.

The first word Moody spoke after regaining consciousness was a grateful: 'Thanks,' as he lay out on his back beside a fire in the lee of a bluff and Colvard spread a blanket over him. And then, a moment later, he added: 'Lieutenant.'

Earlier, while Colvard had been loading the limp trooper on to his horse back at the canyon, the officer had said: 'Fort Benedict is the closest place in any direction where you can get fresh supplies, sir. If I'm not teaching my grandmother to suck eggs as the saying goes. It's what they told me before I left Fort Sully.'

'Stranger in this part of the country, too,' Steele replied. 'Grateful for the information.'

'You're welcome to take a look at my map and go on alone, sir. I'd planned on reaching Benedict by midnight. But with a wounded prisoner and just the one horse, I'm going to be slowed down some.'

He had got Moody in place across the saddle by then: been about to take hold of the reins, but saw the Winchester lying in the dust and went across to it.

'Way your prisoner tells it, nobody should be in a hurry to reach Benedict,' Steele answered.

Then watched as Colvard picked up the rifle by the barrel, swung it back and then powerfully forward, against the rock face to smash the stock out of its mount. Not satisfied with this degree of destruction, he took another swing, to wrench the hammer off and crush the magazine. He then dropped the barrel section across the stock and returned to his horse.

'Won't be of any use to any hot-headed Sioux who happens by now,' he explained.

'Nor any use against any who already have rifles,' the Virginian drawled as the cavalry lieutenant, who was armed only with a sabre and a Colt, jerked on the reins to move the gelding forward.

Which was the sum total of talk between the army officer and the civilian until a few sporadic exchanges later; concerned with the siting, setting up and necessary chores of a night camp. Then, after Moody had been bedded down and was sleeping naturally and comfortably, Colvard filled Steele's and his own tin mugs with the last of the coffee and said:

'I've heard Major McCoy runs a tight fort. But an army without discipline is no army at all. You're of an age to have fought in the Civil War, sir. And if you did, I guess you know I'm talking sense.'

The Virginian had fought in the war. From start to finish. And, like Colvard was, he had been a cavalry lieutenant. But his uniform tunic had been grey. Not for reasons of geography.

Rather because he genuinely believed in the cause of the Confederacy. To the extent that what was left of the Steele family – Adam and his father, Ben – was one of the many which was split by divided loyalties from the moment the first Rebel shell crashed into Fort Sumter one April day in 1861. For, while the son rode away from one of the most prosperous plantations in the state of Virginia, the father chose to remain there in the big house, secretly aiding and abetting Union efforts to crush the South.

It had been a hard and bitter war for Adam Steele, as he put to good military use the hunting and shooting skills he had acquired as a Virginian gentleman of leisure. The kind of war from which, in common with the vast majority of soldiers on both sides, he learned that life was too short and too precious to risk losing it for the sake of an abstract cause. For he saw there was no glory in lying dead in a ditch, blood and slime mingling. And that a man who could look across the churned-up mud of a battlefield and see both his legs lying several yards away did not present any kind of picture of idealism being worth the suffering.

Thus did Steele fight the greater part of the war with survival his sole aim – his own and that of the men under his command. And was prepared, after Appomattox, to forget there had ever been a rift between himself and his father and to seek to re-establish what once had been.

Ben Steele was of like mind and the night of 14 April 1865 was to have been the beginning of a personal peace for father and son. Four years and two days after the attack on Sumter had set them on opposing sides. But on that misty night in Washington, Ben Steele became the innocent victim of a plot by men unwilling to acknowledge peace of any kind. And just across the street from the theatre in which one of their number shot Abraham Lincoln, others lynched Adam Steele's father from a beam in a bar room.

It fell to the son to cut down the body of his father. And to fire the first shot of many which had left his trail from Washington to this night camp in the Dakotas Badlands strewn with the corpses of men who crossed him.

It was not a direct trail and only the first few miles were

18

covered in pursuit of the men responsible for his father's death: pursuit, capture and execution. Punishing them for their crime by means of the Colt Hartford rifle, which was all that could be salvaged from the burnt-out big house back in Virginia. A rifle with a gold plate screwed to its fire-scorched stock, inscribed: *To Benjamin P. Steele, with gratitude – Abraham Lincoln.*

But the war had been over then and the need to assuage a thirst for vengeance was not, in the eyes of the law, an acceptable reason for mass murder. And so it was that a deputy sheriff named Jim Bishop followed Adam Steele out of the east and into the west, intent upon taking him prisoner and bringing him back to stand trial. But with all else worthwhile lost to him, Steele found himself living by the set of standards which had enabled him to survive the war. And since standing trial for a hanging crime was a threat to his survival – and Jim Bishop was too good a lawman to be swayed from his sworn duty – the deputy had to die.

Despite the fact that Adam Steele and Bish had been best friends throughout their childhood and youth.

The trail away from the young deputy's corpse had taken the Virginian to a tiny village in Mexico. Where he lost his taste for liquor during a protracted period of drunken stupor as he sought to drown his remorse over the death of Bish in anything alcoholic which was stocked by the cantina in Nuevo Rio.

From Nuevo Rio – after he had decided that liquor solved no problems and in fact put at risk the life he had killed Bish to protect – the trail had taken him back across the border and zig-zagged, for the most part aimlessly, in every direction and through most of the states and territories west of the Missis-sippi–Missouri. From time to time in the early days there had been personal ambitions beyond the immediate aims of raising enough money to buy the necessities of life.

He had searched for a place to set down new roots, in parts of the country reminiscent of Virginia. Where he might re-establish something close to the kind of life he had looked forward to living when he rode into Washington that April night many years ago.

But always his dreams were dashed and he had finally become resigned to the existence of a lone drifter: destined to ride the wild country, attracting trouble like a magnet draws iron filings. Always surviving by use of his skills learned for sport and developed for war. But seldom winning much more than another day of life. Accepting his lot as fate's punishment – more severe, perhaps, than man-made justice tempered with mercy – for the savage vendetta he had undertaken after the brutal murder of his father.

'I was in the war, lieutenant,' he replied to Colvard's implied question.

'Then I guess you came across officers like Major McCoy? Hard as nails, which makes them unpopular with the men. Until the fighting starts. It's then they prove that discipline pays dividends. In human lives that would be lost if men didn't jump the instant they were told to.'

In the flickering light of the fire, Colvard's rugged features were set in an expression of high enthusiasm.

'Have you done any fighting?' Steele asked.

'Well, no,' he answered, disconcerted. 'This is my first posting. But I had some fine tutors at West Point. War veterans.'

'You don't have to apologise, lieutenant,' the Virginian said. 'Everybody has to learn theory before he can handle the real thing.'

'But it sounded as if you disapproved of my views on discipline, sir?'

An almost imperceptible shrug. 'It's a long time since I was an expert. If I ever was. But I reckon any man who makes judgement on anything without knowing all the facts is riding for a fall.'

Colvard showed doubt. Then vented an impatient snort. 'Major McCoy is renowned throughout this entire Department of the West as a commanding officer who does not lightly tolerate bad soldiers! At West Point he and his methods are put to students as models we should follow. I know this. I also know that Trooper Moody deserted from Fort Benedict. And that desertion from active duty is the worst crime a bad soldier can commit.'

His green eyes gazed fixedly across the dancing flames at the impassive face of the Virginian, challenging the other man to counter this argument.

'You're right,' Steele allowed evenly, rather than electing to prolong the futile discussion. By pointing out that the class-rooms of West Point were far removed from the reality of life in a remote Dakotas fort and that desertion from such a post was not something a veteran trooper like Moody would do for no good reason.

Then, as he prepared to bed down, he sensed watching eyes and glanced across to where the injured prisoner lay under the blanket. Saw that Moody was not, in fact, asleep – and was looking at him with something akin to gratitude in his sunken, exhaustion-circled eyes.

They set out at dawn from the camp, Moody in pain from his injured shoulder which he had to move after many hours of resting in the same position, Colvard weary since he had dozed only fitfully during his watch over the prisoner, and Steele refreshed by shallow but uninterrupted sleep.

Breakfast was of fried jerked beef and beans and coffee, which Steele fixed while Colvard attended to Moody's wound – which was free of infection. Nobody washed up or shaved because there was no guarantee they would reach Fort Benedict on this day and the lieutenant's military map showed no streams or water holes on the shortest route between the bluff and the army post.

Conversation was as lacking today as it had been the previous afternoon and evening: just the few words needed during the noon stop for a meal. Except when Moody, about to be helped by Colvard astride the gelding for the afternoon ride offered:

'Why don't I hoof it for awhile, lieutenant? You're gettin' to look worse than I feel.'

The officer's face – bristled, sweat-run and streaked with dust – abruptly looked as hard and weathered and old as the grotesquely eroded rock formations all around them. 'I told you yesterday, soldier!' he snapped. 'The only time you speak is when you're spoken to!'

Moody seemed about to snarl a retort, but then swallowed

21

his words. But there was still a bad taste in his mouth and he spat forcefully down into the dust after he was in the saddle and Colvard had taken up the reins.

For the greater part of the afternoon, the sun which inched across the cloudless sky was hotter than it had been during the morning. And the three men felt their energy draining out with each bead of sweat squeezed from wide-open pores. The terrain they crossed was arid, hard and almost totally lacking in vegetation. No birds flew overhead and all ground creatures remained out of sight while the trio of men and two horses passed. Heat shimmer veiled distant ridges.

Colvard moved like a sleepwalker. Moody sat erect in the saddle, tense against the chance of falling asleep and toppling painfully to the ground. The Virginian maintained a constant vigilance, as was his custom in open country, small town or sprawling city. Ready to react instantly to the first sign of danger. Alert for any eventuality but on this ride through the Badlands aware of a specific threat. Indians.

For this inhospitable area and the less harsh terrain surrounding it were the homeland of the Sioux. Steele had heard no rumours of any potential trouble but, as Colvard had implied when he smashed Moody's Winchester back in the canyon, there was always a danger that a group of hot-headed braves might go on the rampage against the whites.

But the Virginian's constantly shifting gaze never alighted on anything which caused him to move a hand off the reins to grip the frame of the booted Colt Hartford.

When the heat and harsh sunlight of day gave way to the coolness and glittering moonlight of night, Colvard said:

'I think if we don't stop we can reach the post by one o'clock at the latest.'

'Midnight, lieutenant,' Moody offered. 'I've patrolled this neck of the woods.'

It was obvious he expected another burst of angry words from the officer, but Colvard said, without turning his head: 'You agree we should continue, sir?'

'My rear end can take it if your feet can, lieutenant,' Steele answered.

'It wasn't all theory at cadet training!' the officer responded sharply.

'Friggin' West Point shavetail!' Moody rasped softly, so that only Steele who was riding beside him heard the sour comment.

Encouraged by the knowledge that the end of the long trek was close at hand, and eager to display his stamina to an enlisted man and a civilian, Colvard lengthened his stride. To the extent that the lights of Fort Benedict were in sight before eleven o'clock and the trio were admitted through the post's gateway as the clock above the command office entrance chimed once to mark the half hour.

The fort was built on an area of flat scrubgrass terrain, a mile south of the final outcrop of Badlands rock. Further to the south and to the east and west the quality of the soil improved. Lush grass grew on a series of low rises and there were stands of timber on the slopes. A stream which was a tributary of the White River, meandered in gentle curves among the hills. Within sight of the fort's south-facing gateway there were half a dozen crudely constructed homesteads and perhaps two hundred head of cattle grazing on the unfenced pasture. A well-used trail which began at the fort took the line of least resistance to lead ultimately in a south-western direction.

'Jesus, Arnie, are you in big trouble,' the corporal who swung open the gate rasped after he had thrown up a salute which was acknowledged by Colvard.

'The prisoner has been forbidden to speak unless addressed by me, soldier!' the lieutenant snapped. 'Kindly see that he is locked in the guardhouse to await the commanding officer's pleasure in the morning.'

'Beg pardon, sir. But Major McCoy left orders that he be informed the moment Trooper Moody came back. If he came back, that is.'

'He is back. So carry out the major's orders, soldier!'

The corporal hurriedly closed the gate and went at the double across the drill compound towards a house with a railed stoop to the right of the command office. Colvard led his gelding and the mounted prisoner in the same direction but in less

23

haste. Steele stayed in the saddle as he followed, looking at his surroundings with less interest than the newly posted officer.

Benedict was a large fort, each of its four timber walls about six hundred feet long and twenty feet high. There was a roofed tower at each corner with a Gatling gun mounted in it. Sentry walkways linked the towers and a ladder slanted down to the ground from them. There was a man standing in the moon shadow at each gun and the man who had opened the gate was one of two, armed with .45 Springfield rifles whose sentry positions were on the walkway above the entrance.

All the guards had showed eager but surreptitious interest in the arrival of Moody: curious about the hapless prisoner but anxious not to be seen to be neglecting their duty. Parallel with three of the walls and some ten feet in from them were frame buildings, all of them named by white painted signs.

Under the north wall the command office with the major's house and officers' quarters to one side and the officers' mess, guardhouse and magazine on the other side. The stables, post store and cookhouse were below the west wall, facing across the compound to the barracks block and hospital. To one side of the gate three covered wagons were parked. To the other were four twelve-pounder cannons, their muzzles aimed inwards.

The post was immaculately maintained in every visible detail. From the way the paint on the high flagstaff in front of the command office and the brasswork of the cannons gleamed in the moonlight, to the sharpness of creases in the pants of the sentries and the precise alignment of the parked wagons.

'They were right,' Colvard said with admiration after he had completed his initial survey. 'This is a model of how an army post should look.'

'Kind of place where there's no hot food on windy days,' Steele answered flatly, sensing many eyes watching the newcomers from the darkness behind spotlessly clean windows. Sensing, also, an almost palpable atmosphere of discontent.

'I'm afraid I don't understand, sir,' the weary Colvard said as he completed hand-brushing dust off his tunic and pants.

'Seems to me the major's the kind of officer who'd demand

that even smoke from the cookhouse stack should stand up straight.'

'You sure enough hit the nail on the friggin' head, mister,' Moody rasped.

'Shut your mouth and dismount, soldier!' Colvard ordered, as the door of McCoy's house swung open and the sentry emerged across the wedge of light from the hallway in back of him.

'Major'll be right out, sir,' he said quickly, and hurried on: 'Ain't no unauthorised civilians allowed on the post but I told the major I figured this one was with you and I'd be real grateful if you told him that —'

'All right, soldier,' Colvard cut in. 'Return to your duty.'

The corporal, who was slightly built and little older than twenty, saluted, smiled his relief, shot a pitying glance at Moody who was now down from the gelding, and ran across the compound. He had climbed the ladder and was back in position above the gate by the time Benedict's commanding officer stepped out on to the stoop to cast a flint-eyed gaze over the trio of dishevelled men who stood in front of and below him.

Major McCoy was in his mid-fifties with no hair on the top of his head but a three-quarter circle of bushy greyness around the sides and back. His face was round and fleshy, his evenly tanned skin drawn taut over the bulging cheeks and fat jaw. His grey eyes were widely spaced and slitted. His nose was snub and his mouthline short. The largeness of his ears was more pronounced by the fact that they protruded more than was usual. He was perhaps five feet nine inches tall, evenly and solidly built. Summoned from his bed, he had wetted and towelled his face and donned his pants, hose and shoes. A cape was hung over his shoulders, so that most of his hirsute torso was bared to the chill of the night air.

After a cursory look at the newcomers, he snapped his head to left and right, checking that the sentries within his sight were attending to their duties. Then he fixed his unblinking gaze on Colvard's face and barked:

'Well, lieutenant?'

'Lieutenant Michael Colvard, sir! Posted to your command.'

25

'You were not supposed to be here for another three days.'

The junior officer was already at strict attention. But he was able to jut his chin a little higher in the air. 'I chose to ignore the trail and chance my luck across the Badlands, sir. Cut my time exactly as I planned.'

'You had the luck of a fool!' the unimpressed McCoy countered. 'Your orders indicated you should reach this fort on a specified date. I allow a man under my command just one mistake. Yours has been made. Why is this civilian here?'

The major did not shift his steady gaze away from Colvard's face. As the lieutenant responded to the reprimand merely by a tightening of his clenched fist and a slight reddening of the skin at the nape of his neck.

'His name is Steele, sir. Trooper Moody was firing at him when I happened by. He wounded the deserter and stood guard over him until I was able to take the man into custody, sir.'

Moody, from habit, fear or perhaps in some faint hope that it would serve to lessen the severity of his fate, was standing as ramrod straight as Colvard. The slitted grey eyes of McCoy swept across the trooper's face without showing a sign of anything. And expressed a glimmer of something akin to embarrassment when they met the impassive gaze of Steele's eyes.

'On behalf of the Ninth Cavalry of the United States Army, I tender my apologies, sir,' he growled. 'By his act of desertion he sealed his fate: either to die of deprivation in the Badlands or to be returned here, tried, convicted and hanged. But if you wish to bring charges, they will be added to the indictment to be placed before the court-martial, sir.'

'No charge, major. We traded one hit for three misses. I don't want to rub salt in his wound.'

A curt nod. 'Very well. Then there is no further need for you to remain on this post. If you wish to stay in the vicinity for the night, Mrs Sellers takes in boarders. And I would advise you to spend the night close to Fort Benedict, sir. Some of the local Indians have become hostile.'

'Grateful for the word, major,' the Virginian replied, touching the brim of his hat. 'Where will I find Mrs Sellers's boarding house?'

'The first place you come to on the south trail. You'll find

26

it filthy and stinking but civilians and their property are not within my jurisdiction.'

Steele tugged on the reins to turn his stallion away from the front of the neat, recently painted house.

'Give my best to Gemma Sellers, mister,' Moody asked in a melancholic tone.

'Quiet, soldier!' Colvard snapped.

'You may gather from that it is not just her rooms that the woman is prepared to rent out to a man, sir,' McCoy said disdainfully.

'I'll give her Moody's best is all,' said the Virginian as he started to walk his horse across the compound. 'Never do buy in that kind of Sellers' market.'

Chapter Three

By normal frontier standards the Sellers house looked from the outside to be in a reasonable state of repair. And when the woman opened the door to the sounds of the stallion being halted and Steele swinging down from the saddle, the lighted room at her back showed as poorly furnished with well-used pieces but cleaner than a lot of places where the Virginian had stayed.

The house had obviously started out as a single room shack and additions had been built on over several years and using a wide variety of materials. Thus it lacked the qualities of neatness and order which a man like Major McCoy would find appealing.

The air which spilled with a wedge of yellow lamplight through the open doorway smelled of beef stew, coffee and cigar smoke.

'Evenin' to you,' Gemma Sellers greeted cheerfully around the cigar clenched between her teeth. 'Knew you'd be run off McCoy's Castle so I already turned down a bed for you.'

The cigar looked out of context in her face for she was a handsome woman who, in her late thirties, still revealed in her features strong traces of a former delicate and very feminine beauty. She was a black-eyed redhead with luxuriant hair that grew very long, spilling down her back and reaching to the crests of her large and firm-looking breasts. Her face had the classic oval shape, with high cheekbones, a generous mouth and a fine skin cut with the kind of upward turning lines which suggested a happy disposition. Her lack of height – she stood little more than five feet tall – was emphasised by the fullness of her figure. She wore a high-necked black dress that hugged close to her upper body and arms and fell straight to the floor from the broad curves of her hips.

Steele touched the brim of his hat. 'Arnie Moody asked me to give you his best, ma'am. Appreciate the bed, if it's a single.'

'Poor bastard,' she responded with a brief frown. Then: 'Arnie, I mean. Gettin' caught and brought back here. Bed's a double because they're the only kind I got. Up to my guests whether they want this to be a boardin' house or a bawdy house!'

She laughed, enjoying the joke she had probably made countless times, spat her cigar out on to the trampled dirt and let it burn itself into extinction.

'Two dollars, mister. Includin' a heap of stew tonight and ham and beans for breakfast. Feed and water for your horse in the stable out back. Stew'll be on the table when you get through beddin' him down. Just walk right in. Nobody around here stands on ceremony. Outside of McCoy's Castle that is.'

She closed the door, which shut off a pleasant stream of stove heated air as well as the light and cooking smells. Which encouraged the Virginian to waste no time in leading his horse around to the rear of the house and into the stable which was across a yard flanked by shade trees. There was just one horse – a black gelding – already enjoying the equine comforts of shelter, clean straw, sweet water and fresh oats.

As Steele returned to the front of the sprawling, single-storey house, he sensed the eyes of the fort sentries upon him: directing resentment and envy through the moon bright night. Rancour, too, perhaps – for the hand he had in bringing Moody back to face McCoy's ire.

'Drop it down anyplace for now and eat your food,' Gemma Sellers called from the rocker to one side of the glowing range fire. 'Show you the room later. Though ain't much to see.'

Steele stacked his saddle and bedroll against the wall by the door, with his coat and hat on top. And was conscious of his

29

two day growth of bristles and the dust clogging his pores and streaking his forehead as he sat at the centrally placed table.

'Guess you was told I'm Gemma Sellers?'

'Adam Steele,' the Virginian supplied before he tasted the first spoonful of stew and decided he was about to eat the best meal he had had for a very long time.

'Used to raise cattle when my husband was alive. But the Sioux got him one day a couple of years ago. When we went to bring back one of our cows they snitched. We was doin' all right, but cowpunchin' ain't for a woman on her own. So I started to take in boarders. But ain't many strangers pass this way, unless they be army men and they stay at the castle. Could've got married again. To any one of a dozen men that asked me. Army men. A couple of them officers. But though I ain't of an age yet when I can live without a man, never did meet one who could fill my John's shoes.'

As she spoke, rocking gently back and forth in the chair, she gazed up ruefully at a crude oil painting which hung on the smoke-stained wall above the range. A portrait of a man with a black beard, broad nose and high forehead.

'John knew of my needs,' she went on, and now shifted her gaze towards Steele. 'And he ain't disapprovin' of what I do. Makin' life a little more bearable for the men from McCoy's Castle. Keepin' from goin' out of my mind myself. And eatin' regular.'

'People have to get by the best way they can, ma'am,' Steele said to fill the expectant pause she made. 'Bonus when they enjoy their work.'

She nodded her appreciation of his attitude towards her way of life. 'What line of business are you in, Mr Steele? You look like a drummer, but you don't carry no samples.'

'When I need the money, I do what's available,' the Virginian replied.

'But a travelling man?'

'I don't get to stay in one place for too long,' he allowed.

She sighed. 'I hate to turn away business, but I wouldn't advise you hang around this part of the country too long. Not unless you have to.'

'I reckoned just to rest up the night, ma'am.'

'Even that could be too long, mister.'

'The Sioux?'

'You got it. Rumour is, they're up to here' – she touched the side of a hand to her throat – 'with the way McCoy's been ridin' herd on them like they was a bunch of scraggy long-horns. And if they get hot enough under the collar about that, they'll hit Benedict real hard. Anythin' and anybody who's in their way as well.'

Steele set down his spoon on the empty plate, his belly full, his body warm and his eyelids heavy.

'You want a smoke?' Gemma Sellers asked, lighting a fresh cigar.

'Don't use tobacco, ma'am.'

'A snort?' She reached down beside her chair and raised a bottle of rye and a glass.

'Don't use liquor, either.'

'And I ain't your type of woman,' she said evenly, smiling through the drifting blue haze. 'It's lucky you enjoy your food and appreciate a soft bed, Mr Steele. Or I'd be takin' your two bucks under false pretences.'

'I have another couple of weaknesses, ma'am.'

'What are they?'

'Coffee and staying alive.'

There was a coffee pot on the range and a row of six tin mugs hanging from hooks to one side. She waved a hand to indicate these and then the chair, across the hearth from her, which had the upholstery showing through several splits.

'Help yourself, mister,' she invited. 'And then be on your way if you've a mind. Fifty cents for what you and your horse have eaten.'

Steele poured himself a mug of coffee and lowered his rump gratefully on to the chair. 'Seems to me, if the local Indians are getting restless, the best place to be is close to an army post.'

She coughed on the cigar smoke and snorted. 'I'd agree with you, mister. If the post wasn't McCoy's Castle at this particular time.'

'Was only in Benedict for a few minutes, ma'am. But it looked to have enough men and firepower to handle anything the Sioux could muster.'

She nodded. 'That's right, it does. But that's right now. And sure enough, if the local Sioux came this minute, the boys at the fort would give them somethin' to remember. But every minute they don't come, McCoy's gettin' closer to bein' lynched and the boys takin' off every which way.'

'Moody didn't set a very good example, ma'am. He got caught. And if he hadn't been, he'd have died from exposure.'

'Lot of them figure the risk is worth takin', Mr Steele. And with no officer left to send out search patrols, they wouldn't have to take the Badlands route.'

Gemma Sellers was no longer pretending an indifference towards the Indian threat and the uneasy situation at Fort Benedict. Some of the lines in her face had a downturn now and the anxious frown made her look older and less handsome.

'Moody expects to be hanged,' Steele said.

She nodded and for a moment chewed her lower lip. 'I know. There's not much that happens behind that stockade I don't get to hear about. Most of them who come here just need me as a woman. To others I'm a kind of mother figure, I guess. The only person around here they can talk to. Rest of the homesteaders don't like the army men. With good reason. Never was much trouble with the Sioux before Benedict was built.'

She paused again, but in no expectation of a response. She merely glanced up at the bad picture of her former good husband and recalled distant memories. Then she sighed, tossed her part-smoked cigar into the range fire and took a first sip at the rye.

'If McCoy does try to string up Arnie Moody it could be just what's needed to start the mutiny. Soon as he was found to be missin', McCoy sent out patrols every which way. With orders to bring him back alive so he could be court-martialled and hung. Which didn't go down well with the men on account that Arnie's a very popular boy. McCoy even led one of the search parties himself. And it was his bunch had a run-in with half a dozen braves. Killed five of them. For no good reason is what the Sioux say. Worst beatin' they've had since Benedict went up.'

'If you've heard rumours that it got the Indians fighting

mad, the men on the post must have heard the same thing, ma'am.'

'Sure they have, mister,' she said, her voice rasping now. 'But them that figure to put pay to McCoy and take off know they'll be all through with the army. So why would they want to risk their necks fightin' for the army first?'

The Virginian nodded in acknowledgement of her sound reasoning. Then, as he finished the coffee, he asked: 'Doesn't McCoy or any of his officers suspect there's trouble brewing?'

Her frown altered to a sneer. 'That straitlaced sonofabitch doesn't know what it's like not to be hated. He figures it's the secret of his success. I never get to entertain his officers. Just know there ain't been no accusations so far.'

Steele eased upright from the chair, having relished its comfort and the warmth of the range fire. But now that his creature requirements had been filled and his curiosity about potential trouble was satisfied, the promise of being able to stretch out full-length on a bed between crisp sheets had a stronger appeal.

'Through that door and then the one facing. There's a basin and pitcher on the bureau. Cold water. If you need hot tonight, you're welcome to use this fire. Pump out back in the yard.'

'Too bushed to bother, ma'am,' he said as he crossed to get his gear from beside the front door. 'You don't mind me dirtying up the linen?'

'Part of a woman's work is cleanin' up after a man, Mr Steele. You take them off when you go to bed?'

'Ma'am?'

'The gloves? You ate with them on. Sat by the fire . . . ' She shrugged. 'I just wondered.'

'Wear them from habit, Mrs Sellers. It started way back in the war. For a long time now they've been something like a lucky charm. Used to put them on when there was trouble. Come so I wear them most of the time now.'

A nod and a knowing expression. 'When I realised you couldn't be a drummer, I figured you were that kind.'

He halted by the door in the side wall of the room. 'What kind is that, ma'am?'

'Oh, there's no name for it. Like butcher or baker or candlestick maker. Not a gunslinger. Kinda like an army trooper, but without a uniform and without no one over you to give you orders. But maybe a . . . yes, a soldier: soldier of fortune.' She looked at him sharply and quickened her speech. 'No offence, Mr Steele. In times of bad trouble men like you can be better to have around than the boys in the fort.'

'No offence taken,' he told her. 'Like I said earlier, people have to get by the best way they can.'

'I'm mighty glad to have a man like you in the house to-night. Even though that sonofabitch says he'll allow civilians on to the fort if the Sioux come. Way things are shapin' up, could be we'd have a better chance makin' a stand right here. What do you think?'

She shivered, as if a sudden draught had sneaked in under the door and streaked across the room to touch only her.

'I don't know ma'am. I'm a soldier of fortune. Not a teller of.'

Chapter Four

There were drape curtains at the window of the small room in which Steele slept. But the window faced east and the first rays of the new day's sun easily penetrated the threadbare fabric of the curtains. To lance against his eyelids and trigger him awake.

He woke, as usual, to instant and total recall. In the unfamiliar room with the familiar Colt Hartford within sight and easy reach where it leaned against the wall beside the bedhead.

Several cocks were crowing, making the only sounds within earshot until the bed-springs creaked under him and then his bare feet padded on the bare floor as he crossed to the window. He drew aside the drapes and eased up the window. The air of sunrise was pleasantly warm and redolent with the aromas of grass and pine trees and cows. Uniformed figures moved in the south-facing towers and on the walkway above the entrance of the fort. A flock of birds flew across the sky above the leading arc of the red-tinged sun. Smoke lifted lazily up into the infinite blueness from two stacks behind the timber wall of the army post. The homesteads within his range of vision from the window showed no signs of life beyond the post-dawn stirrings of domestic animals and fowl.

As he washed up and shaved, using the cold water from the pitcher, the rest of the house continued to be clamped in silence. He used the razor carefully, for there was no mirror in the room. There were no frills at all in the room: just the bed, the bureau with three empty drawers, the basin and pitcher and a kerosene lamp which hung from a hook in one white-washed wall. But the place had served his purpose adequately.

While he was dressing – he had stripped down to his long-johns for bed – a hammering sound began to disturb the peace which had previously existed beyond the confines of the spartanly furnished room. First just one man beating a hammer-head against nails. Then three of them. This set cattle to lowing for a while all over the vast area of rolling pastureland. Cooking pots clattered for a few seconds somewhere in the Sellers house.

Steele pulled on his pants, which had a neat slit in the outside seam of the right leg: this giving him access to the wooden-handled knife which he wore in a boot sheath. And the last item of apparel he donned was also a weapon – the grey silk kerchief which he hung around his neck. For this had weights sewn into the fabric at diagonally opposite corners which made it an Oriental tool for strangulation. Forerunners of the knife predated the Colt Hartford, for he had taken to carrying such a concealed weapon during the war. The lethal scarf was taken from a dark-skinned killer while he was closing in on the murderers of his father.

He went out into the main room of the house, lugging his saddle under one arm and his bedroll and top clothes beneath the other. The appetising aromas of frying ham and brewing coffee filled the warm, brightly sunlit air.

Gemma Sellers turned away from the range, looking weary and haggard, as if she had not slept during the night. But she wore a fresh dress, styled the same as the black one, but white.

'Oh,' she said as Steele came through the doorway. She brushed hair off her face. 'I didn't think you'd be up. I haven't done anythin', short of startin' breakfast.'

He understood her discomfiture, for he had felt something similar when he entered her house, unshaven and with a day's dirt ingrained in his skin.

'Most important thing for me right now, ma'am. Smells good.'

'But I don't and neither will the house until I've cleaned both of us up. I hate it when this place starts to look like what McCoy tells men it's like. Here.'

There was a place laid at the centre table. She put down a plate of food and a mug of coffee. Then carried a kettle of steaming water out of the room. Steele ate his breakfast as the hammering from the fort continued. Except for a sixty-second interruption during which, through the window and without moving from the table, he saw the stars and stripes rise up the final few feet of Fort Benedict's flagstaff.

'Was that racket that disturbed you, I guess,' the woman said sourly as she returned to the room. Her hair was brushed to a tidy sheen and the ravages of a restless night had been camouflaged by soap and water and the skilful application of paint and powder. But the means to bring sparkle back to her black eyes lay in her mind behind them: and if she had tried to find the key, she had failed.

'Wake with the sun. Always have.'

She went to the rocker, unhooked a mug on her way and poured coffee. 'Be the buildin' of gallows for Moody I shouldn't wonder.'

'You won't see the hanging,' Steele pointed out.

She shook her head. 'But I'll know when it happens. And I know enough about army ways to know it shouldn't happen. There's no war on. All that should happen to Moody is a ball and chain for a month or so. Even if there was a war, he oughta be shot, not hung.'

'It won't matter to him, ma'am,' Steele replied as he stood up, took two dollar bills from his pants pocket and dropped them on the table beside his cleaned plate. 'The rope is as fast as a dozen bullets if it's done right. And I'd guess Major McCoy does everything to perfection.'

Now her eyes gained life, as she snapped her head around to stare angrily at the Virginian. 'I'm nothin' more nor less than a whore, mister!' she snarled. 'But I know what honour means! And hangin's a lousy, stinkin', rotten way to die for a man that don't deserve it!'

'Same as getting blasted by a thirty-eight-forty bullet from a Winchester in the middle of the Badlands, Mrs Sellers,' Steele replied as he went to the door.

'Arnie tried to —' she began and broke off, shocked. 'I let him have that rifle after he got out of the Fort.'

'He reckoned he had good reason to shoot me, so I don't wish him no ill will,' he replied, cracking his eyes against the full glare of the now-yellow sun. 'But then I don't have a whole lot of sympathy for him, either. Grateful for your hospitality, ma'am.'

He pulled the door closed behind him and made a brief survey of a greater area of lush Dakotas grazing land than had been visible from the windows of the house. As yet, all human activity except for the ceaseless guard patrols on the fort walkways was concealed by stout walls.

Inside the post, the troopers and their officers made many subdued sounds which contributed to a general hubbub of talk and movement to counterpoint the steady thud of hammerheads against nails and timber. Occasionally, a horse snorted or a man's voice was raised, sharp but indistinct.

Only smoke, rising from stacks to smudge the clear blueness of the morning sky, showed that people were up and about in the scattered houses.

Elsewhere, cattle grazed, birds flew, penned pigs and goats and chickens and milk cows made known it was feeding time. A lone dog yapped incessantly.

Then, as Steele turned to start for the stable behind the Sellers house, a new feature showed on the landscape. A covered wagon which crested a rise perhaps a mile and a half out along the trail to the south west. By the time he had saddled his well-rested stallion, lashed his bedroll in place and led the animal out into the sunlight, it was possible to see two other wagons behind the first – flatbeds which were heavily laden. All three were halted in front of the most distant homestead, the driver of the lead wagon talking to a man and a woman from the house. Then the vehicles started to roll again, dust billowing up from beneath wearily clopping hooves and slow turning wheels.

Steele swung up into his saddle and rode the horse to the

side of the trail in front of the Sellers house.

'It's begun,' the redheaded woman said ominously from the threshold of her home, holding a hand to the side of her head to keep the sun out of her eyes.

'You know those people?' Steele asked.

'Never seen the covered wagon before. But the other two – they belong to the Ivetts and the Mandersons. And that looks like . . . yes, that's Mr and Mrs Rosenberry.'

She was referring to a pair of riders who showed on the trail where it crested the most distant rise. A very tall man and an enormously fat woman whose unusual physiques made them stand out despite the fact that they were still at least a mile and a half away.

Behind them a pony and a trap came into view. Followed by a small buckboard. Behind this, a group of half a dozen people on foot. These were joined by the couple from the house where the wagons had been halted – the man carrying three valises which he loaded on to the already highly stacked buckboard. The woman led a small white terrier on a leash.

News of the approaching convoy of civilians was shouted down into the fort by the gate sentries and the hammering was curtailed. First one officer and then three more appeared on the walkway, to train sun-flashing field-glasses on the advancing group: which swelled in size as people hurried from the homesteads, carrying suitcases, valises and hastily gathered bundles of belongings. One old man dragged on the bridle of a reluctant milk cow.

With one hand still shielding her intently staring eyes from the sun, Gemma Sellers unfolded fingers away from the other as her lips moved in a silent count.

'All except two,' she announced at length. Softly, to herself. Then, to Steele: 'Do you see anyone carryin' a baby, mister?'

'No, ma'am.'

The woman groaned. 'The Rambachs, then. They only got here three months ago. Blacks that most people didn't welcome. So they set up home six or seven miles to the south in an old buffalo hunter's shack. I helped deliver Emmy's daughter. Second day they got here.'

The lead wagon neared the house, driven by a harassed

but self-important-looking middle-aged fat man with thick-lensed eye-glasses.

'Hostile Indians!' he called as he drove his weary team close enough to Steele and the woman to make himself heard above the creak of timbers and clop of hooves. 'Hit the house of a nigra family off to the south! Made me sick to my stomach what them savages done to the nigras! Little baby, too!'

Then he was by the house, and shouting up to the troopers and officers on the walkway to open the gates of Fort Benedict. Most of the people behind him pointedly ignored Gemma Sellers. Except for the old-timer who was breathless from the exertion of leading the now-co-operative cow at a half run to draw close to the head of the column.

'Get what you value and bring it to the post, Gemma!' he urged, spittle spraying from his mouth with the words. 'McCoy's really stirred up the Sioux this time! They're comin' this way!'

'She sits on the only assets she's got, Clem!' the tall, gaunt-faced man driving the buckboard hurled down sourly as he drove by. As the equally thin woman at his side sniffed.

'Up yours, preacherman!' Gemma Sellers shrieked, then shot an embarrassed sidelong glance at the mounted Virginian. 'Said that because he ain't really an ordained minister, mister. What's called a lay preacher.'

'And I reckon you never did,' Steele replied with a wry smile as he jerked on the reins of his stallion and clucked the horse into movement. Turning to the right to head along the south west trail, against the human tide which was coming to a halt behind the covered wagon stalled at the closed gates of Fort Benedict.

'You gotta be crazy . . . '
'Them Injuns mean business . . . '
'The liquor drummer saw what they done to the Rambachs . . . '
'Grown ups and the little one, too . . . '
'Them savages know they won't get away with that . . . '
'Now they done that, they gotta go all the way . . . '
The stale news and the warnings were shouted, rasped and

whispered croakily to Steele as he rode slowly along the column of wagons, people on horses and those on foot. Middle aged and elderly most of them, but with a half dozen young couples among their number. No children. Anxiety, quaking fear, anger, deep shock, frustration and self-pity were the predominant emotions expressed by the sweating faces of the homesteaders.

At first, the Virginian touched the brim of his hat when a woman spoke and muttered an even-voiced 'Grateful to you,' to the men. But then he ignored all of them and soon was beyond the back markers. But still close enough to Benedict to hear, indistinctly, the shouted exchanges between men at the head of the column and the officers on the walkway above the fort entrance.

After a night of rest and with a full belly, the black stallion was eager for exercise and Steele gave the animal his head, steering him to keep him on the trail. He only reined him in as the horse started up to the crest of the rise where the drummer's covered wagon had first come into view.

By then, other riders were on his back trail. A bunch of six uniformed figures who had emerged from the fort and had the gates slammed closed behind them.

At the ridge, Steele halted his mount and looked down a long, broad, low-sided valley. The sun was high enough now to be above the eastern slopes, shafting down its brightness to sparkle on the surface of the shallow stream which flowed due south before it and the valley curved south west. Perhaps two miles away. The trail followed the almost arrow straight line of the stream.

In the valley, the homesteads were not scattered. Instead they were built close to the trail and water course at about quarter mile intervals. Just as in back of where Steele sat his stallion, a few hundred head of cattle roamed at will over unfenced grazing land. Narrow tracks, the grass trodden down by horses and men on foot, meandered up the valley sides in many places. Only the blue sky was visible above the grassy, timber-featured ridges to east and west. And even as the Virginian watched, a shimmering heat haze began to veil the southern section of the valley. Smoke wisped from some of the homesteads stacks, but many abandoned cooking fires had already burned out.

Steele did not look around as hooves beat the earth behind him, harness creaked and metal jingled.

'What do you see, sir?' Lieutenant Colvard called above the lessening noise as the riders reined in their mounts.

'A fine piece of cattle-raising land,' the Virginian replied and glanced at the men who steadied their horses to either side of him.

Colvard, looking immaculate except for old sweat stains on his uniform tunic. And a sergeant and four troopers without a detail McCoy would be able to criticise about their personal freshness and uniform smartness. The non-com in his forties, the enlisted men all about the same age as the officer. There was a bright eagerness about Colvard, in his expression and the way he leaned forward in his saddle, raking his field glasses over the terrain in front of and below him. The sergeant was impassive. The troopers appeared strangely depressed.

'What do you think, Sergeant Floyd?' Colvard asked. 'You know this country.'

'Sure I do sir,' the non-com answered dully, and came close to sighing, but held back when Colvard allowed the field glasses to dangle around his neck and looked hard at him. 'And it's my opinion that we're short-handed for the job the major give us.'

'The country and the hostiles, sergeant!' Colvard snapped. 'Your opinion of our commanding officer's orders is of no interest to me!'

Floyd still retained a very faint trace of Irish accent in his voice. He was six feet tall and probably weighed more than two hundred pounds. Big bones and solid flesh, that of his face stained dark ochre by sun and wind. He had permanently narrowed blue eyes and a too-short, thick-lipped mouth. His iron-grey hair was cropped as close as that of Moody and the four disconsolate troopers in this group. At first impression he looked like a man slow to anger but hard to subdue once his ire was ignited. Now he revealed his resentment of the newly-posted officer by a short-lived pulsing at the side of his neck.

'To the east and west the country's a series of valleys like

42

this one, except there ain't no streams in them, sir. South of where this one swings to the right there's a plain that's mixed scrub grass and thick timber. The Rambach place – the one the whisky drummer says was hit by the Sioux – is just around the curve where the valley swings out of sight beyond the heat haze.

'No Injun brave smart enough to get to be chief would bring his warriors up this Barton River Valley. On a direct line for the post. He'd advance from the east or the west. But you send men up on the ridges, all they'll see is another valley either side of this one. From the next ridge it'd be the same. For a thorough reconnaissance, you need twenty men, lieutenant. Each with semaphore flags or a heliograph. One on each ridge. Spot the Injuns coming in on us at the front or circlin' around to hit us from out of the Badlands.'

'You're getting close to complaining about the major's orders again, sergeant!' Colvard warned grimly. He turned in the saddle and stabbed a manicured finger at two of the troopers. 'You and you. We'll scout the west side of the valley. Floyd, you will cover the east side.'

'Sir,' the sergeant acknowledged, then scowled at the back of Colvard as the lieutenant spurred his horse down from the head of the valley. Then the expression was expanded to a glower as the slitted blue eyes raked to the Virginian's face. 'Why don't you ride on out mister,' he invited bitterly. 'I'd like for the Sioux to have some of their kinda fun with you after you helped bring in Moody.'

'Many more feel that way, it could be I'll stand more chance out there with the Sioux, feller. What I hear.'

Floyd spat phlegm at the ground. 'Gemma Sellers has got a big mouth,' he snarled.

'For which some of us are very grateful,' the thinner, blond-haired trooper put in, and showed a leer that grew into a giggle.

'Get your friggin' mind up from between your stinkin' legs, Cass!' the non-com snapped in controlled fury. Then, to Steele: 'You're not stupid enough to ride out there alone, mister! So bear this in mind when Major Friggin' McCoy lets you and the rest dirty up his castle with your civilian boots . . . you say one word out of place —'

43

'Floyd!' Colvard bellowed as he halted before the climb up to the western ridge, his rage clear to hear in the quiet heat of the morning air. 'Follow your damn orders, man! Move out!'

'Frig off, bastard!' Floyd muttered, but jerked on the reins and nodded for Cass and the other trooper to start down the south-facing slope. Then looked back over his shoulder to rasp at the Virginian: 'I guess you've heard enough to get my drift, mister?'

'Not a matter of drift, feller,' Steele drawled, tone even but dark eyes glittering dangerously from out of the shade beneath his hat brim. 'Seems to me you're sailing . . . pretty close to the wind.'

Chapter Five

Despite Floyd's rancour towards him and Steele's resentment of the sergeant, the civilian respected the cavalryman's assessment of the situation in the event that the attack on the negro settlers was not an isolated incident.

The Virginian had ridden up to this vantage point to check on the kind of terrain which lay beyond the rise. And it was his good fortune that he overheard Floyd's description of the kind of country which lay on the other side of the distant ridges. Country in which the whole Sioux nation could hide and over which it could advance in secret: unless more than a handful of sentries was deployed to the best advantage.

A lone rider would need far more than his fair share of luck to run that kind of gauntlet. And if he had no good reason to take the chance, he would be a fool undeserving of any luck at all.

On the other hand, the local homesteaders might have over-reacted by abandoning their places and livestock to seek the protection of Fort Benedict. Maybe the attack on the Rambach family had been carried out by a small party of hotheads: in retaliation for the slaughter by McCoy's patrol or for some quite different reason. The negroes' homestead selected because it was the most isolated. Such a band would be on the run now, blood-lust satisfied or eager to enjoy the spoils of their victory.

Lieutenant Colvard put Steele's thoughts into words as he and the grimly taciturn Floyd rode back along the trail to the army post, the Virginian riding between the two cavalrymen. The four troopers had been left to keep watch on the settled Barton River Valley and the flanking depressions.

As they neared the end of the line of abandoned vehicles – all the settlers had gathered into an angry group before the firmly closed gates of the fort – the frowning officer finished voicing his reflections upon the Sioux raid and its ramifications and put sharpness in his tone to allow:

'I'll put your suggestions regarding more pickets to Major McCoy, sergeant. I also feel a patrol should be dispatched to investigate the scene of the attack.'

The offer did nothing to ease the aggrieved mood of the non-com. 'The major's been known to listen to suggestions, lieutenant,' he growled.

'You see anythin' out in the valley?'

'They comin' yet?'

'You tell McCoy he's gotta let us in.'

'Yeah, it's his duty to protect the civilian population.'

The questions and demands came thick and fast from the jittery group of men and women gathered beside the covered wagon of the bespectacled liquor salesman.

'Stay calm!' Colvard urged, holding up a hand to quieten the anxious and angry voices. 'As yet, everything appears quiet but we —'

'Lieutenant!' McCoy bellowed from the other side of the gate. 'I give you any order about reporting to a bunch of civilians? Get in this fort! Open that gate, trooper!'

The furious commanding officer of Benedict was obviously in a position to see beyond the stockade: for as one of the gates was creaked open a crack and the gaunt-faced lay preacher led a forward surge by the civilians, he snarled:

'Shoot any unauthorised person who attempts tresspass!'

There were four troopers, a lieutenant and a captain on the walkway above the entrance. The enlisted men clicked back the hammers of their Springfield carbines as the officers drew and cocked their Colt .45 revolvers.

The ominous sounds of metal against metal caused the

advance to halt. And shocked eyes were raised to stare incredulously at the downward canted barrels of the guns. Colvard and then Floyd rode through the wider opened door, which was immediately closed behind them.

'This is nothing short of disgusting!' the unordained man of God blurted.

As the cigar-smoking Gemma Sellers, who had not moved away from where she leaned against a front wheel of the covered wagon, said to Steele: 'Guess the army boys didn't see any more than you, mister?'

The fifty or so other men and women shut out of the fort all turned their attention to the still-mounted Virginian.

'Nothing,' he supplied.

'What?' From the six feet six inch tall man with the grossly fat wife.

'No sign of any Indians,' Steele augmented.

'Well I sure saw some signs, mister,' the liquor salesman yelled, pushing through the crowd, sunlight glinting on the thick lenses of his eye-glasses and on the sweat beads that hung in the bristles of his bulging cheeks and fleshy jaw. 'A nigra with maybe a dozen arrows in his chest and belly! A naked nigra woman with her breasts cut off! And a baby not three months old without a head!'

'Stop it!' a woman shrieked. 'Please stop it! I don't want to hear any ...'

She was a pretty brunette of about twenty, who covered her ears with her palms as she fell into the embrace of her dull-faced husband.

'Yes, Mr Clarke,' the preacher snapped as the woman's words were lost to a bout of body shaking sobbing. 'We have already heard your vivid description of the scene of the raid.'

'If the Sioux don't wanna be seen, they won't be,' the old-timer named Clem muttered. 'Real sneaky Injuns, the Sioux. Why, I remember one time back in '62 when —'

'Your reminiscences of times past have no relevance to the present situation, Mr Burns,' the preacher said.

'It ain't often you talk sense, Preacher Boucher,' Gemma Sellers growled as she sent the stub of her cigar spinning to the side of the trail. 'Just hope you aren't about to start one of your sermons.'

'A prayer to the Lord might not be amiss!' the painfully thin Mrs Boucher said to everyone in the crowd. Then fixed her glassy-eyed stare on Mrs Sellers. 'Even your soul may not be beyond savin' if the worst happens!'

'If the worst happens, lady!' the part-time whore rasped, 'it could be that folks who practice christian charity might be ahead of them that just sermonise about it when we get to the pearly gates!'

Footfalls rang on the boards of the walkway above the gate and McCoy's head and shoulders showed above the pointed tops of the pine trunks that formed the stockade.

'You people!' he bellowed as the crowd mumbled responses to Gemma Sellers taunt: to silence the noise and draw all attention towards himself. His slitted grey eyes surveyed the group as if the men and women were a herd of scrawny cows and he was an experienced cattle baron used to dealing only in the best beef. 'I'm going to allow you inside Fort Benedict.'

'Thank God,' the fat wife of the very tall man gasped.

'Be quiet and listen!' McCoy went on as others started to voice their relief and gratitude. 'You will be offered the protection of this post for as long as it takes Lieutenant Jennings to lead a patrol to the Rambach shack and return here with a full report. Whether I extend the privilege of Benedict's facilities to you civilians will, of course, depend upon what the lieutenant has to report.'

'We understand that, major,' Boucher responded eagerly. 'None of us wish to be away from our homes and land unless there is a real threat of Indian attack.'

McCoy slammed his right fist into the open palm of his right hand, a redness of mounting anger spreading across his tanned skin. 'I said to be quiet and listen!' he roared, glowering down at Boucher, who bristled and tried in vain to out-stare the commanding officer of the fort. McCoy nodded his satisfaction with the silence. 'There are conditions: which every one of you must abide by or face the consequences. This fort is military property and while you are on it, you will be subject to army regulations. Which means, quite simply, that you will all do what you are told, how you are told, when you are told. Is that understood?'

Several people nodded, but McCoy stared only at Boucher. 'You, sir!' he snapped, 'I will consider to be in charge of all civilians. Responsible for ensuring that whatever orders are passed down the army chain of command are carried out. Understood?'

'Certainly, major,' Boucher replied without enthusiasm. And then shared a resentful glance between Gemma Sellers and Adam Steele.

This was not lost on McCoy, who added:

'Breeches of discipline among the civilians will be reported to the officer of the day, Mr Boucher. Who will refer them to me.' He ensured that his menacing eyes raked across every face in the crowd. Then he yelled: 'Trooper, open the gates! No vehicles or animals will be admitted!'

'What about my little Jojo?' the slightly built, elderly woman with the white terrier on a leash cried. Then stooped to pick up the dog and hold it to her flat chest. Jojo licked her face affectionately.

'Dogs do not defecate in the latrine!' McCoy snapped, turning away from the stockade as the gates were drawn open.

'But he'll die if he's left out here to fend for himself, major!'

'Then have somebody shoot him, lady!'

'I'm not going in! I'm not going in without Jojo, George.'

While she argued the point with her husband, the other homesteaders and the liquor drummer crowded through the gateway into the immaculately maintained fort. McCoy was already halfway across the compound by then, passing the almost-fully-constructed gallows at the centre and heading for the area in front of the command office where an elderly lieutenant and a corporal and six troopers were astride their mounts. The men and horses looked smart enough to stand guard of honour outside the Capitol in Washington.

Equally well turned out were the troopers engaged in routine post duties, most of which seemed to be concerned in maintaining Fort Benedict at its high standard of gleaming cleanliness.

4   49

A snap of the major's fingers and un upraised arm sent four men back to the chore of completing the gallows.

This as the captain and two sergeants organised the civilians into haphazard ranks of three.

Steele saw all this from glances he shot through the open gateway as he dismounted from the stallion and began to unsaddle the horse. Watched, with more than a hint of scorn in her black eyes by Gemma Sellers.

'You gonna turn him loose, mister?'

'Like to put him back in your stable.'

She shrugged. 'Help yourself. But I'd figured a man like you wouldn't want to be too far separated from his horse.' Now she looked through the gateway to where McCoy was talking fast to the tense looking lieutenant in charge of the patrol. 'Nor the kind to take easy to what a hard-nosed army major says. When all it amounts to is pullin' rank for the lousy sake of it.'

'He's the boss, ma'am,' Steele told her as he rested his gear against the wheel of the covered wagon on which she was leaning. 'Of everything inside the stockade. And my horse won't be any use to me in there.'

The woman straightened up. 'Take Mrs Peachey's dog along with you, uh? Tie him up in the stable. Maybe put down some of the cold stew left over from last night.'

'Sure,' the Virginian agreed.

'Oh, thank you, thank you,' the elderly woman blurted. 'And perhaps we'll be allowed out later to give Jojo more food, Mrs Sellers?'

'You folks comin' in or stayin' out?' one of the sergeants organising the civilians called wearily. 'Captain Starling's ready to fill you all in on what you gotta do and not do while you're on the post.'

'Come on, Dora,' Mr Peachey urged, tugging his wife up from where she was crouched, kissing the head of the excited terrier.

'I'll let you know if you miss out on anythin' real excitin' while you're gone,' Gemma Sellers told Steele wryly as she trailed the elderly couple into the fort.

This as the veteran Lieutenant Jennings commanded his

patrol to move out. And Steele started away from the post gateway, leading his horse by the bridle and Jojo by the leash. Unbidden. Clem Burns's milk cow fell in behind the stallion and the dog. While the saddle horses and those in the traces of the wagons remained where they had been abandoned, docile and doleful: the sweat of flight drying on their coats in the hot sun of early morning. The clock in the fort began to chime the hour of eight just before the clop of hooves of the patrol's mounts drowned out the sound.

Back in the fort, two men in punishment fatigues doubled forward to sweep up droppings which one of the horses had deposited on the compound.

'You plannin' on settin' up a zoo, Steele?' one of the troopers on the patrol detail rasped as he rode by. And remained grim-faced while the other troopers and the corporal guffawed their appreciation of this latest attempt to needle the man who had helped bring in Moody.

'Short a few animals, feller,' the Virginian drawled.

'Maybe we'll bring you back some that are real savage – the kind with red skins!' a trooper growled.

'Or maybe the Sioux will make monkeys out of you.'

'Silence in the column!' the front riding lieutenant yelled and everyone except him glared resentfully at Steele.

The little white terrier sneezed in the dust raised by the hooves of the horses as they broke into an ordered canter.

Steele grinned boyishly down at the bright-eyed, tail-wagging Jojo. And said: 'Seems like the army's putting both of us in the doghouse, boy.'

Chapter Six

The forty-year-old pot-bellied and sad-eyed Captain Starling had finished reading out the riot act to the civilians by the time Steele got back to the fort after taking care of his horse, the dog and Clem Burns's cow. But the gates were not yet closed. For the newcomers to Benedict were allowed to fetch their personal possessions from the wagons and to set free the horses which had brought them to the fort.

By the time this was done and every civilian had been allocated a supply of bedding and twenty-four square feet of floor space in the mess-hall, the gallows at the centre of the compound was finished. And the clock above the command office doorway showed the time of a quarter of nine.

As they stood in the doorway of the mess-hall, watching disgruntled troopers polish the artillery pieces, clean windows, paint woodwork and sweep building stoops, Gemma Sellers told the Virginian the gist of what Captain Starling had said to the civilian guests. All of it was reasonable, the rules designed to keep the non-military personnel from hampering the routine running of the post. Even the woman objected strongly to just two of the regulations – no smoking until after sundown and no drinking liquor at all.

While he listened to her and watched, with apparent indifference, the resentful troopers carry out their menial chores – only those posted on the south wall walkway looking for signals from the pickets on the distant ridges were intent upon their tasks – the Virginian noted the absence of officers. Also, that the embittered Sergeant Floyd was nowhere to be seen.

Behind him, in the crowded mess-hall converted to a make-shift barrack, the tension eased as the local civilian population relished the comparative safety of the post. At the same time as, out in the harsh sunshine or in the hot shade of other fort buildings, the atmosphere became more highly charged with each passing moment.

It was possible to see, as they worked, that most of the troopers shot frequent anxious glances towards the façade of the command office. But just as apparent – to anyone with a modicum of ability to sense a threat of impending trouble – was the fact that even more pairs of disgruntled eyes were looking from many places of concealment towards the door-way beneath the clock.

'That gun's as much a part of you as the gloves, ain't it?' Gemma Sellers said thoughtfully after a pause of perhaps a full minute.

Steele was leaning his left shoulder against the doorframe and the Colt Hartford was canted carelessly to his left, a hand fisted around the frame.

'Value it almost as much as my life, ma'am,' he replied. 'And one has saved the other lots of times.'

'You figure you're gonna need it when the court-martial's over?'

'That what all the officers are up to?'

'Looks like. Soon as the patrol left, McCoy had Moody brought out of the guardroom and into his office. By Lieutenant Dunbar and the new shavetail. Then Captain Starling went in there.'

'The man's a fool.'

'He sure is,' Gemma Sellers replied to the short, fat, ugly-featured man who had stepped silently into the doorway between her and Steele. 'You won't find many people around here to disagree with you, Mr Ivett.'

The fifty-year-old homesteader who had driven one of the flatbeds up to the fort had a thick, black, drooping moustache. He ran his yellowish tongue over the sweat beads in the bristles. 'He'll need every soldier he's got if the Sioux hit us. What's

53

his damn hurry? He could've waited.'

The mess-hall had become quiet and a new, almost palpable tension had insinuated itself into the hot, sweat-smelling atmosphere of the place. Everyone, sitting, kneeling or lying on the unfurled bedrolls, gazed anxiously at the doorway, listening to the exchange between Gemma Sellers and Ivett.

'We are guests here!' the lay preacher put in grimly as he rose to his feet and swept his hard-eyed stare over the people around him. 'Unwelcome guests. It will do us no good at all to interfere in military business.'

'I agree, I agree,' the liquor salesman named Clarke said eagerly, rubbing the condensation of his own sweat off the lenses of his eye-glasses.

'Our instructions could not have been plainer,' Boucher went on. 'We must do nothing to hamper the daily routine of the fort.'

'McCoy didn't lay down no law about us not talkin', preacherman,' Gemma Sellers growled. 'And there ain't nothin' routine about a secret trial and them gallows that makes the verdict a foregone conclusion. How say you, Mr Steele?'

'Reckon nothing any of us can say will alter what's going to happen,' the Virginian replied as the clock began to strike the hour of nine and the door beneath it opened. 'Matter of how far McCoy reckons he can push the men on this post.'

'That is none of our business!' Boucher countered, his tone rising. 'And I consider that the way you are standing there with that rifle is provocative. I order you to put it away!'

Moody, trying hard to conceal his fear of death behind a sneer of contempt, stepped out of the doorway. Close behind him, hands draped over the butts of Colt revolvers in unfastened holsters, were Colvard and an older, less-confident-looking lieutenant – Dunbar. Then came the sad-eyed Starling and bringing up the rear was the grimly satisfied McCoy. The two senior officers were armed only with cavalry sabres. All the men were in full campaign dress uniforms except for Moody, who was hatless. The prisoner's hands were behind his back, apparently tied at the wrists.

'Don't nobody move a muscle!' Sergeant Floyd roared. As

he stepped from the doorway of the post store, a Springfield carbine levelled from his left shoulder to draw a bead on the major.

This a moment after McCoy had ordered the prisoner and escort to halt, some six feet in front of the command office. As satisfaction was displaced by angry suspicion – his slitted grey eyes having seen nothing abnormal about the post, but his sixth sense for danger warning him that all was not well.

Designated men did not obey the order of the now stock-still Floyd. As, up in the corner towers, the four multi-barrel Gatlings were swung on their tripods and angled down to aim at the compound. And other troopers and non-coms stepped from doorways with cocked carbines pressed to their shoulders, muzzles trained on the group in front of the command office.

One man – the short stockily built corporal who had opened the gate last night – had a different target. From the threshold of the stables he drew a bead directly across the compound at the Virginian.

'Seems you've been countermanded, feller,' Steele said.

'Damn right!' one of the two corporals growled as the double-doors which connected the mess hall with the enlisted men's barrack were flung wide.

These men also had carbines which they raked back and forth over the shocked, gasping, quaking civilians.

'Got 'em, sarge!' the second corporal yelled, loud enough for his voice to carry out into the compound and across it.

'Only what Sergeant Floyd says goes now,' the other man in the double doorway rasped. 'And he says any of you people cause trouble, we gotta blast you.'

'Drop your hands away from them revolvers, lieutenants!' Floyd ordered.

'And you toss the rifle out in front of you, Steele!' the corporal in front of the stable demanded.

'Move forward, Moody!' This from Floyd, as Colvard and Dunbar snapped their heads around to seek a sign from McCoy.

Fear, emanating from those with aimed weapons as well as those covered by them, seemed to have a heavy physical presence in the bright, hot air. Which pressed down upon the heads and shoulders of everyone in the fort: to squeeze great beads of salt sweat from their pores.

Moody vented a low moan and lunged forward too fast. He tripped over his feet and pitched to the hard-packed ground: screamed in agony as his wounded shoulder was jarred.

Floyd altered his aim and triggered a shot. The bullet tunnelled into the compound between the booted feet of Colvard and Dunbar.

'Do it!' the sergeant roared as the echo of the gunshot resounded between the façades of the fort buildings.

While, displaying his respect for the Colt Hartford, Steele dropped slowly down on to his haunches, placed the rifle gently on the ground and pushed it forcefully away from him. Stock first.

Moody yelled and bellied awkwardly but fast across the compound.

Colvard and Dunbar leapt instinctively sideways and dropped their right hands off the butts of the holstered revolvers. Which left the quartet of officers in an uneven line, the two lieutenants a pace in front of McCoy and Starling.

Dunbar and the captain looked drained and wan, completely shocked by the act of mutiny. While McCoy and Colvard, though grim-faced, were totally in control of their emotions. Whether afraid or enraged or a mixture of the two.

The major had started to issue a soft-voiced command to the two lieutenants. Now he spoke loud enough for his voice to carry to every part of the fort, his slitted eyes fixed upon the menacing form of Floyd, his voice even in tone.

'Hear this! Whatever the outcome of this insurrection, the ringleaders will suffer the ultimate punishment!'

'We hear you but we ain't listenin', Major Friggin' McCoy!' the corporal who was covering Steele yelled. 'Let's get him strung up right now, sarge! Let's string up all the lousy stinkin' officers!'

'Easy, Sibley!' Floyd roared, and there was a trace of anxiety in his voice and attitude as he canted the Springfield to his shoulder and raked his blue eyes, narrowed as much as those of McCoy, over the face of every man and woman in

56

sight. 'Everyone take it easy. Jordan, cut Moody's hands free! Sibley, Hardy, Girling, Kupperman, disarm the officers and lock them in the guardroom!'

Jordan – a youthful-looking corporal – ran out of the cook-house, drawing a knife from the back of his belt.

'What about Steele, sarge?' Corporal Sibley wanted to know. 'Him, too? He helped the new shavetail bring in Moody, didn't he?'

Three of the men detailed were already closing in on the line of officers. Coming out of McCoy's house with levelled Colt revolvers. Sibley continued to keep his carbine aimed across the compound at the Virginian.

'Steele's okay, sergeant!' Moody called as he was helped to sit up by Jordan, who then started to saw at his bonds. 'And so's Lieutenant Colvard. They was good to me.'

'Sergeant, I don't like none of this!' one of the troopers above the gate complained. 'Don't you count on no help from me!'

'Nor me!' a man working in the magazine augmented. 'This ain't right! Especially not now the hostiles are on our damn doorstep!'

'Any man who stands by and does nothing will be regarded as guilty as —' McCoy started.

'Shut up, all of you!' Floyd snarled. 'Everyone do like I tell you! Won't be no killin' – no one strung up! Not if them that ain't with us don't move against us!'

'But, sarge —' Sibley began.

'Shut your friggin' mouth!' Floyd shrieked as he whirled to look at the eager-to-kill Sibley. 'I told you, damnit! All we need to do is keep Moody from bein' hung and see to it headquarters knows what kinda officer McCoy is! Any killin's and we're sunk!'

Sibley muttered his discontent under his breath, but relaxed his vigil on Steele and moved out across the compound to where the three other troopers were gesturing with Colts for the officers to head for the guardroom.

Floyd shifted his attention towards the walkway on the south-facing wall. 'Any man who ain't for seein' justice bein' done better come down from there!' he yelled. 'I don't want no one tippin' our hand to Jennin's when he brings the patrol back here!'

One trooper looked at three others and received the tacit agreement of one of them. They headed for the closest ladder.

'All right!' the leader of the mutiny shouted, his head moving constantly from side to side to direct his words in every direction. 'The men that have their orders will carry them out! All other military personnel will go into the enlisted men's barrack! The civilians will stay right where they are!'

As he finished speaking, he fixed his menacing stare on Steele, Ivett and Gemma Sellers who filled the mess-hall doorway. Then he started across the compound, his stride purposeful and his face hard set. The carbine was still sloped to his shoulder and every other man on the ground had lowered his gun. But the Gatlings mounted in the corner towers continued to menace every square inch of the fort's interior.

'Sergeant, I must protest!' Boucher said in a severe tone as he came on to the threshold and peered out between the heads of the woman and Ivett.

'Sorry you people had to get mixed up in this,' Floyd said. 'But we had to do it just now to keep McCoy from executin' Trooper Moody.'

'But we are in danger of imminent attack by God knows how many savages!' the lay preacher insisted as Floyd came to a halt.

'I know it.'

The gaunt-faced man moved forward, knocking Gemma Sellers and Ivett aside: to step out into the sunlight and glare at the sergeant. 'And have seen to it that the men capable of countering such an attack are incarcerated! A most stupid act if I may —'

At close quarters, in the harsh brightness of the mid-morning sun, it was possible to see in the slitted eyes and weathered skin of Floyd the high degree of strain he was suffering.

The uniformed man, who had successfully organised a mutiny and quelled an attempt to make it something more than bloodless, was perhaps conscious of several troopers and noncoms looking at and listening to the confrontation at the mess-hall doorway. And maybe realised that something more than mere words was needed to entrench his position as leader. Or perhaps it was a purely personal requirement – that he had reached a point where he needed a physical outlet for the tension.

Whichever, Boucher was too incensed to take the time to consider what the look on the other man's face might signal. And did not curtail the stream of hard-spoken words until Floyd started to move. Which was too late.

The sergeant whipped the Springfield barrel away from his shoulder, took a two-handed grip around the frame and swung the carbine viciously to one side.

Boucher rocked backwards from the waist with a cry of alarm. But the side of the barrel cracked against his temple, splitting the skin. So that as he slammed to the ground, his profile was curtained with blood.

'Eddie!' his emaciated wife shrieked, and tripped to pitch forward across the unfurled bedrolls as she sought to reach the doorway. 'You've killed my husband!'

'You want to check him out, Steele?' Floyd said, sloping the carbine to his shoulder again. Then he raised his voice: 'You soldiers inside, keep everyone in there!'

'Sure, sarge!'

'Hold it, lady!'

The carbines of the two troopers in the barrack doorway swung to left and right again.

As the Virginian stepped forward and dropped into a squat beside the curled up form of Boucher.

'Preacherman still in business?' Gemma Sellers asked bitterly.

There was just a slight rise and fall of the gaunt faced man's chest, but with a gloved hand on the side of his throat, Steele was able to feel a strong pulse.

'Not souled out yet,' he reported.

Chapter Seven

In less than thirty minutes from the moment he stepped out of the post store and aimed his Springfield at Major McCoy, Floyd had totally secured his command of Fort Benedict. For, by using their fear of the threatened Indian attack, he gained the co-operation of almost everyone on the post – soldier and civilian alike – in accepting that somebody had to be in charge and there were no other contenders.

Only two men – both troopers – felt strongly enough about the wrongness of the mutiny that they demanded to be locked in the guardroom cells with the officers. Other dissenters made known their objections but promised allegiance to Floyd until the Sioux threat was dealt with or proved to be empty.

During that time, as the unconscious Edward Boucher was carried to his bedroll, had his wound bathed and dressed by a hospital steward and gradually returned to awareness of pain and depression, the big-built sergeant with iron-grey hair told the civilians to continue to obey the regulations outlined by Starling: then toured the fort to check that his forward planning was being put into operation. After this, he installed himself in the command office and held a briefing session with two other sergeants – Scott and Durrell – and Corporal Sibley.

Steele, his Colt Hartford returned to him – only the men in the guardroom had been ordered to surrender their arms – went up on to the walkway of the south-facing wall. Where the youthful-looking Corporal Jordan was in charge of the sentries. The redheaded squint-eyed Trooper Hardy manned the south-west-corner tower and the portly Trooper Kupperman was behind the Gatling in the shade of the south-east tower. Moody, the scars of sunburn healing, but pale from the effects of facing being hanged and suffering fresh pain from his recent fall, shared the gate sentry duty.

All the cavalrymen posted on all four walkways were now able to concentrate fully on their designated task – to watch for the first sign of hostile activity on the terrain which surrounded Fort Benedict. To the south, east and west: pleasant pastoral vistas across which cattle and a few loose horses moved, listless in the mounting heat of morning – cropping at lush green or drinking from the slow-running water of the stream. Northward, the ominous line of barren and jagged ridges which marked the start of the Badlands. With the naked eye and through the magnifying lenses of field glasses the men scanned the distant horizons, which were brought closer by the moist-looking sheen of heat shimmer. Often, the men had to run a tunic sleeve over their foreheads or purposely blink to keep the sweat beads out of their eyes.

'Hell of a thing,' Moody said after a long period of silence.

'What is?' Jordan asked. He was at least five years younger than the trooper's thirty and still grew fuzz rather than bristles on his pleasant but weak-looking face.

Moody licked his lips with a tongue that was still tinged with yellow, and nodded down at the line of abandoned vehicles parked in front of the gates. 'Guess I ain't the only man around here with a powerful thirst. And there's a wagon-load of liquor out there.'

'Get it out of your mind, Arnie!' the younger man snapped, his face unable to match the grimness of his tone. 'You were in the guardhouse when Floyd was plannin' to take over. But you heard what he said awhile back. Headquarters is gonna get to hear what's happened. And if we don't run Benedict the army way, it's gonna be worse for us than servin' under McCoy.'

'Yeah,' Moody said without enthusiasm, and spat down over the top of the wall. 'Floyd always did go by the book, same as the friggin' major.'

'He saved your damn neck, Arnie!' Jordan countered vehemently. 'So you got no call to insult him that way! Jack Floyd's army through and through! But he ain't never gone along with treatin' men like tin soldiers, workin' them until they drop then puttin' them on punishment detail for havin' dirty uniforms and bein' too damn tired to drill like the book says!'

'I ain't sayin' —' Moody began.

'And he sure wasn't gonna go along with you bein' hung after that crooked court-martial you was put through!'

Moody worked a grin across his narrow, angular features. And shared it between the irate Jordan and the impassive Virginian. 'All I was sayin' was that it seems a waste – all that liquor being left outside.'

The corporal was not mollified. 'Say it too loud, Arnie, and some men without reason to be grateful to Jack Floyd might hear you.'

He glanced down at the compound with the unused gallows at its centre and the neatly kept buildings surrounding it. All the chores designed to keep Benedict looking spick and span had been curtailed. Apart from the sentries on the walkways and the noncoms planning strategy in the command office, the only other men working were in the stables and cookhouse. All others were in the barrack block beside the mess-hall, resting.

'You could still face court-martial, feller,' Steele pointed out. 'With a firing squad or ten years' hard labour at the end of it. If it turns out this post is in a state of war with the Sioux.'

'We know that,' Jordan rasped with a grimace. And shot anxious glances along the walkway at Hardy and Kupperman. 'Jack Floyd made sure some of us knew it. But I'd thank you to quit that kind of talk, mister. And I don't want you spreadin' it around, Arnie.'

Moody showed a broader grin. 'In case some of the boys figure we might as well get hung for a sheep as a lamb? Thanks, Steele. I'll bear it in mind.'

The Virginian nodded. 'One way of looking at it, feller. Mentioned it because I reckoned you might like to make a deal with McCoy and his officers.'

'Set 'em free and all'll be forgiven?' Moody sneered.

'Men have made their point and you escaped hanging,' Steele answered evenly. 'You saw a little of the kind of man Colvard is when he was bringing you in.'

'Not in a million years, mister!' Jordan growled. 'I know what you're gettin' at. Floyd and some of us even thought about doin' thin's that way. But we figured if we did anythin', it had to be all the way.'

'You got my vote for that,' Moody said harshly. 'But I'd like to see it go even further. I'm with Leon Sibley. We oughta string up Major Friggin' McCoy. Then maybe burn his damn castle to the ground. And take off so the friggin' army couldn't touch us. Who needs the stinkin' Ninth Cavalry, anyway?'

His voice got louder as his anger rose. Men on all the walkways looked towards him. Others – and a few women in the mess hall – peered up at him from windows and doorways below. Some expressed nervousness and other faces were set in pensive frowns.

'Quit the talkin' and attend to your duty, Moody!' Jordan ordered. And glared at Steele, blaming him for bringing up the subject 'And you get back to the mess-hall, mister. You got no right to be up here!'

Steele nodded his acknowledgement of the truth of this and moved along the walkway to climb down the ladder. As he neared the doorway of the civilians' quarters, the elderly Clem Burns called:

'Any sign of the Injuns, mister?'

'No, feller.'

'We have less to fear from the Sioux than the vicious men who have gained control of the fort!' the thin Mrs Boucher growled from where she sat on the floor beside her pale-faced husband.

The doors connecting with the barrack were now closed and there were no soldiers in the mess-hall. Most of the homesteaders, weary from the morning flight to Benedict and shocked by the events which followed, sat or lay on the army-issue blankets. Drained and uneasy. Flanking the old-timer with the spittle-run chin were Gemma Sellers and Clarke, the liquor drummer. The woman was smoking a cigar, encouraged to break the tobacco edict by the fact that a haze of blue smoke drifted from out of the door and open windows of the barrack. The pompous-looking salesman continued to sweat a great deal. Burns nodded sagely.

'Mrs Boucher could be right,' he said as Steele elected to sit on the ground in the shade with his back against the wall to the right of the doorway, rifle gripped between his knees. 'Until nightfall, anyways. If them braves that hit the Rambach place was just a bunch of young bucks they'd have done one of two things. Come on down the valley full tilt or taken off.'

'And they didn't come beyond the black people's place, Mr Burns,' the grossly overweight Mrs Rosenberry said eagerly.

'That's right!' Dora Peachey agreed and turned to her husband. 'It could be safe for us to go home, George. Get Jojo and go home. Away from this terrible —'

'But maybe it wasn't just eager-beaver young bucks,' Burns cut in on the slightly built, ten-years-his-junior woman. 'Maybe it was a half dozen warriors hand-picked by old Chief Lone Horn. To hit the Rambachs the worst way there is. Scare the shit – beg pardon, ladies – scare all us folks real bad and set us runnin' for Benedict.'

'Oh, dear God,' the pretty brunette Mrs Manderson cried.

'You are doing nothing to ease our troubled minds,' Edward Boucher chided Burns.

'Let him tell it, preacherman,' Gemma Sellers growled. 'Clem's been out here for long enough to know the Sioux better than most. Could be he'll steer us into doin' somethin' a whole lot more useful than prayin' to save our necks.'

'I ain't tellin' no one what to do!' Burns put in quickly. 'Just sayin' what I think about how old Chief Lone Horn'll play thin's, if he's behind what happened to the blacks.'

'Go ahead,' Gemma invited.

Now that the old-timer was conscious of having a much larger audience of listeners than those in the doorway, he became reticent and his voice was a growling whisper.

'Well, the Sioux they don't like gettin' killed, same as we whites don't. And the way the valley's settled, a whole lot of

64

braves would get to reach the happy hunting ground if they came full tilt along the river. On account of the fact that soon as the shootin' started way down at Stan and Iris Ivett's place, rest of us and the army would have time to get ready for them.'

'Nonsense, Clem,' the unusually tall Rosenberry countered. 'We're even more ready for the hostiles now. All of us together and better protected in the fort than alone in our homes.'

'Right now we're good and ready, Tom,' the old-timer allowed. 'But it's broad daylight on the first day. We got night to come. Then another day and another night. Guess you know what I'm drivin' at young feller?'

Steele glanced up into the shrivelled face of Clem Burns. 'Floyd's the one you should be talking to, feller,' he drawled.

The old man showed an almost toothless grin. 'Jack Floyd's about the one good thing in this whole sorry mess, mister. He's less than half my age, I figure, but there ain't nothin' I can teach him about the Sioux and the way old Lone Horn thinks. If McCoy had've listened to the sense Jack Floyd had to talk about the Sioux, we wouldn't all be cooped up here like chickens when a fox's about now.'

The post clock struck ten times and everyone in the mess-hall listened in tense silence to the mournful chimes: realising exactly what it was that Clem Burns was driving at before he got sidetracked into singing the praises of the new commander of the fort.

Time would pass and the Sioux were a patient people. Who could afford to let the time pass as they closed in, under cover of darkness across terrain rich with pockets of concealment, on an enemy conveniently huddled together in one place. A stronghold, certainly. But one in which the passing of time would take its toll on those who defended it. In terms of alternate periods of high tension and boredom within the claustrophobic confines of the stockade taking the edge off readiness.

'Damnit, they could even starve us out!' the ugly Stan Ivett exclaimed, tongue darting to lick sweat off his drooping moustache. 'There are twice as many people in here as usual!'

'Thirst would get us first,' Burns pointed out. 'And you can bet your bottom dollar old Chief Lone Horn'll make sure we can't get to the river.'

'Stop this kind of talk!' Boucher demanded, folding up into a sitting posture and directing a glare in every direction. 'All it amounts to are ifs and buts. Which cause unnecessary distress. Whatever happens – and perhaps the hostiles will not come – we are in the hands of Sergeant Floyd. And as far as he is concerned, I am in agreement with Clem Burns. Whatever else he may be, the sergeant is an expert on the Sioux and their ways. And known personally to the chief. If there has to be fighting – or there is an opportunity to prevent bloodshed – we could not have a better leader.'

'Yeah,' Gemma Sellers growled through teeth clenched to her cigar. 'All them redskins'll toss away their weapons and think it's a sign from the Gods. When Jack Floyd drops his pants and they see the sun shinin' outta his ass!'

'Shut your foul mouth, woman!' Boucher hurled at her.

'Quiet on the post!' the new commander of Benedict yelled as he emerged from the doorway beneath the clock, trailed by Sibley, Scott and Durrell. 'Wake up everyone that's sleepin' and listen!'

While the other three noncoms stayed on the ground – Sibley glowering and the two veteran sergeants impassive – Floyd climbed up on to the gallows. Disconcerted by the noose hanging so close to his head, he swung it viciously so that the rope coiled several times around the strut. Then:

'All right! Hear this! Until the patrol led by Lieutenant Jennin's get's back, we've got no way of knowin' whether or not the Sioux are fixin' to hit us! Maybe we won't even know then! But we gonna be good and ready for the Indians if they do come! And if they don't, then the hard work won't have harmed any of us!'

He went on to reveal the defensive plan which had been worked out in the command office. Then designated noncoms to organise work details of troopers and civilians which would implement the various aspects of the plan.

When he was through and the fort came alive with noise and movement, Gemma Sellers trod on the remains of her cigar and growled: 'All that sun comin' out of his ass, I guess the crap has to come from someplace else.'

'What Floyd do to you, ma'am?' Steele asked as he got to his feet.

'Tried to have my place put off limits to the boys,' she muttered vehemently. 'Reckons that soldierin' and women don't mix.'

'You, you and you,' Sibley snapped, stabbing a finger at Steele, Burns and Ivett. 'Help move the wagons!'

'You amaze me, mister,' the woman said with a shake of her head as Steele made to move off in the wake of the older men who hurried to follow Sibley. 'Man like you, doin' everythin' Floyd says!'

'Everything he's said so far has made sense, ma'am,' the Virginian answered evenly.

'You'll be kissin' his ass next!'

'No, ma'am. Always try to keep the sun out of my eyes.'

As he joined Sibley's detail in moving the wagons into a semi-circular line of defence twenty yards away from the south-facing wall of the fort, Steele decided he knew why Gemma Sellers's mood had deteriorated during the course of the morning. At first he thought it had been enforced abstinence from tobacco. Then, as he heard bottles rattling while the heavily laden wagon of Clarke was hauled into the line, he thought that the need for rye was probably the prime cause of her irritability.

He also noted that the sound of glass clinking against glass set the troopers who were helping to manhandle the wagon to thinking about what was in the bottles.

When the wagons were in position, supplemented by the three army vehicles from inside the fort, three of the twelve-pounder cannons and a supply of shells were placed behind them.

Another work detail hauled the other artillery piece and several rounds of ammunition out to the Sellers house where they were set up in the stable.

To the rear of the fort, a rope corral was erected and a dozen head of beef cattle were driven into it.

While a human chain of women transferred pail after pail of stream water into every kind of container in the cookhouse.

Beyond this centre of frantic activity, a dozen uniformed figures rode out in various directions, all of them armed with carbines and some carrying field-glasses. Each with a day's rations in his saddlebags and canteen. To relieve the pickets Colvard had detailed earlier in the day and to provide Benedict with the kind of forward sentry positions which Floyd had told the lieutenant was necessary.

Not enough, but there could never be enough. 'Chief Lone Horn can muster more than two hundred braves,' the sergeant had announced from the gallows. 'Countin' civilians, we have less than a hundred and fifty. If he attacks in force we have to even up those odds real fast. And if he puts us under siege, then we have to make sure we can hold out for as long as it takes to needle him into closin' in!'

By midday all the preparations were complete and the fort was quiet in the blistering heat of the sun. The four troopers who had held down picket duty at the head of the Barton River Valley were all agreed that Floyd did the right thing in taking over the post. So none of them joined the quartet of officers and the two troopers in the guardhouse. The happiest person in Benedict was the slightly built, sixty-year-old Dora Peachey who had been allowed by Floyd to bring her dog from the Sellers house. But perhaps the terrier had preferred the stable, for he constantly followed Steele around or lay at his side: recalling that the Virginian had taken him to the less-crowded and cooler place.

Between noon and one o'clock there was constant, low-key activity as troopers and civilians filed into and out of the cookhouse to be fed. Then, until mid-afternoon, peace and quiet reigned again. It was the pretty, black-haired Mrs Manderson who commented that Gemma Sellers had not returned to the mess-hall after going to the cookhouse.

And Tom Rosenberry, his long frame sprawled on his blankets, growled: 'We should be thankful for small mercies, Janet. Without liquor inside her, that woman is insufferable.'

Edward Boucher snorted. 'Her ill humour has more to do

with the fact that she is surrounded by so many men and is unable to —'

'You people oughta be ashamed of yourselves!' Clem Burns accused. 'None of you got any idea what it's like for Gemma after her husband died the way he did! Her being left in that big house, lonely and —'

'Keep your voices down!' a man called. 'Some of us are tryin' to get some sleep!'

There was a chorus of agreement. Then a few more complaints as Steele moved out of the mess-hall, his boots scraping on the floorboards, this sound counterpointed by the pitter-patter of Jojo's paws.

He swung to the right and sauntered across the front of the barrack, which was noisy with the snores and deep breathing of sleeping men, past the silent hospital and then turned left towards the façade of the guardhouse and magazine which shared a common door. To one side of this was a blank wall behind which arms and ammunition were stored. To the other, a single-barred window.

Colvard's square, ruggedly formed face showed at the bars. 'Hell of a thing, Mr Steele,' he said.

'Floyd's done everything he should,' the Virginian answered, looking beyond Colvard into the overcrowded cell.

There were just two cots in there. On one of them, the sad-eyed Captain Starling, the fiftyish, almost bald lieutenant Dunbar and the two troopers in their early twenties sat in a close-packed row. Like Colvard, they had taken off their tunics and unfastened their shirts at the throat. But they still sweated, their faces run with salty beads and their clothing stained by great, dark patches of moisture.

On the other cot, Major McCoy was sprawled out full length on his back. He had removed only his hat and he had his hands linked under his head as he stared fixedly up at the ceiling. His round, fleshy face was set in an expression of intense loathing. His voice was thick with the same emotion as he said:

'Sergeant Floyd has signed his own death warrant, mister!'

'What's the feeling out there, sir?' the thinner of the two troopers asked anxiously. 'I know there's some others who ain't with Jack Floyd.'

'Men more intelligent than you two!' McCoy snarled through clenched teeth. 'Who realised they can do nothing locked in here!'

Both men sat to rigid attention, staring at the wall above where the major lay, while he spoke.

'Well, sir?' Colvard asked Steele.

'From what I've seen and heard, lieutenant, most people like what Floyd's done to secure the post against Indian attack.'

'The Sioux will not attempt to take Fort Benedict!' McCoy countered. 'Unless they learn that I am no longer in command!'

Only by a brief scowl of contempt did Colvard reveal how he felt about the major's contention. Then he said: 'Most people, sir?'

'There are a few who are as unconcerned about the Indian threat as the major,' Steele replied.

'Men like Corporal Sibley?' Colvard asked tautly.

'You heard him at the start of this.'

'Sibley will face the same punishment as Floyd!' the major rasped. 'Likewise the Sergeants Durrell and Scott. They are the ringleaders.'

'Pardon me, sir,' Colvard said with clearly detectable impatience. 'But such threats are futile in the present situation. I think we should try to take advantage of —'

'Take care, lieutenant!' McCoy snapped, screwing his head around to direct an angry glare at the junior officer. 'I still consider myself the commanding officer of Fort Benedict. And as such will take note of every example of insubordination which I will deal with at such times as —'

'The hell with that, major!' Lieutenant Dunbar muttered. 'Right now you're no more in command of anything than that cockroach on the damn wall!'

McCoy folded his back up from the bed, swung around and slammed his booted feet to the floor. 'Consider yourself on commanding officer's report, lieutenant!' he bellowed.

'Sure thing, major,' Dunbar replied wearily and threw up a negligent salute. Then vented a short, harsh laugh. 'You want Captain Starling to place me under closer arrest?'

'Easy, Gerry,' Colvard placated.

'My God, my officers, too!' McCoy rasped as he raked his slit-eyed stare over their faces.

'Sir,' Starling said nervously into the tense silence. 'No disrespect intended, but this line of talk is getting us nowhere.'

McCoy brought his temper under control. 'So what do you suggest we discuss, captain?' he asked sourly.

Starling licked his lips and looked helplessly at Colvard.

'Perhaps the reason for Mr Steele's visit?' the most level-headed man in the cell said.

'Just passing by,' the Virginian replied to the implied query. 'Looking for Mrs Sellers.'

'You disgust me!' McCoy snarled, and threw himself out on to his back again. 'At a time like this thinking of —'

'Why, sir?' Colvard interrupted.

'She has a drinking problem which she may have solved, lieutenant.'

Colvard was perplexed for a few moments. Then realisation flooded across his sweat-run face. 'The wagon of the liquor salesman!'

Steele nodded as McCoy sat upright again and joined everyone else in staring hard through the bars at the Virginian. 'I reckon most people forgot what was aboard Clarke's wagon in all the excitement. But a few men heard the bottles rattling when we moved the wagons.'

McCoy came up from the cot and approached the window. He clenched his fist around two of the bars and gazed into Steele's face with intense pleading. 'You have to find her, mister! And get rid of whatever whiskey's left. Get Floyd to detail some men to help look. In the event that woman is sharing the liquor. If enough men get drunk enough . . . My God, all hell will break loose on this post!'

'Sir!' Colvard rasped, leaning to the side so that he could look across the corner of the compound beyond Steele.

The Virginian had already turned, as he heard a latch lifted and a door creak open.

'Too late,' McCoy growled. 'That as well.'

That was the blatant invitation to sexual pleasure which Gemma Sellers extended. As she stepped unsteadily out of the hospital doorway and staggered to a swaying halt six feet away from the threshold. For she was stark naked: only her face partially concealed by long strands of red hair that were pasted by sweat to her flesh. Other patches of hair grew at her armpits and at the base of her belly. Elsewhere, the bright afternoon sun blazed down on white flesh featured with large circles of pink at the crests of her sagging breasts and a number of angry-looking bruises and scratches on their slopes. The freshly made marks of brutal passion.

She stood with her legs splayed wide and belly pushed forward. After a moment, she threw her arms to the sides and pulled her shoulders back: which had the effect of taking up the slackness from her breasts so that they became firmer and thrust forward. Then she shook her head violently and her hair fell away from her face. For stretched seconds she blinked against the sunlight and seemed confused as she raked her gaze over the façades of the surrounding buildings.

Captain Starling peered out of the barred window between McCoy and Colvard.

'You think she's drunk?' he asked in a hushed whisper.

Steele took a tighter grip around the frame of the Colt Hartford sloped to his shoulder and drawled: 'She's sure too big to be lost.'

Chapter Eight

'Anymore of you sonsofbitches want to have a real woman?'
Gemma Sellers roared after she had almost toppled to the
ground, struggled to stay upright and recovered from her
initial confusion. 'I've about finished off the boys back there!'

She extended a thumb from a clenched fist and jerked it
towards the hospital doorway.

Within moments of beginning to shout the words which
augmented the provocative stance of her naked body, the
woman had drawn every eye towards her. The men on guard
duty upon the walkways, other soldiers who peered from
windows or spilled out of doorways and the civilian population who crowded out from the mess-hall. And Sergeant Jack
Floyd who came to a halt, grim-faced and rigid, on the threshold of the doorway under the clock.

'Come on, come on you beautiful men!' Gemma yelled,
swinging to left and right from the waist so that everyone was
able to see her lust-scarred body. 'Form a line and see what
you can do to —'

Many of the men in uniform began to whistle and cheer and
shout their willingness to accept her challenge.

Several of the women from the mess-hall screamed their
shock and some berated their husbands and tried to force the
men back to where Gemma would be hidden from them.

Floyd, quivering with rage, jerked the Colt from his holster, aimed it into the air at the full reach of his arm and triggered off a shot.

The report curtailed the din and now all attention was swung towards the furious noncom.

'Get back inside there and put some clothes on!' he snarled. 'Everyone not on guard duty, clear off the compound!'

He wrenched his gaze away from the wantonly displayed body of the woman to rake it around the fort. Then glared again at her as she began to taunt him.

'Up yours, Floyd! Just 'cause you ain't man enough to raise it, no reason to deny real men their fun!'

She started forward, unsteady on her bare feet, hands cupped over her hips, breasts tremoring as she moved.

Floyd was momentarily lost for words or a course of action. And looked away from the woman as if searching for a solution to his quandary.

'Hey!' the trooper manning the Gatling on the north-west corner of the fort stockade called shrilly. 'She's liquored up! Where'd she get the liquor?'

'The drummer's rig!' a trooper in the stable doorway supplied. 'Liquor's his business! I told you guys I heard —'

'Do as you been friggin' well told!' Floyd shrieked, a mixture of rage and fear driving his voice to a peak of shrillness.

He swung the Colt, no longer aimed at the cloudless sky, and men ducked or stepped fast into cover: afraid that in his present state of mind the sergeant might fire the gun by accident.

'Back him up, Steele!' Colvard hissed through the bars. 'If he loses control —'

'Be lucky if that's all he loses, feller,' the Virginian drawled as all attention was switched away from Floyd and the naked woman towards bleary-eyed, half-dressed men who emerged from the hospital doorway. Sibley and Moody. The red-haired and squint-eyed Trooper Hardy and the portly Kupperman. Three other enlisted men who had been on the detail assigned to move the wagons. None of them wearing boots and some naked above the waist. All of them carrying Springfield carbines held two-handed but slanted down to aim at the ground. No one as drunk as Gemma Sellers, who came to a halt and

74

fell on to all-fours as she turned to look back at them.

'We gotta have a talk, Jack!' Sibley called across the compound, a hard expression on his thin face.

'You bastard!' Floyd accused him.

And made to swing the Colt towards the corporal. But halted the move as seven carbines were levelled at him, across the woman who gasped her awareness of the crossfire danger and sprawled out on the sun-baked ground, face down.

'Careful, Jack!' Sibley warned and abruptly seemed sober. 'I don't want for no one to get hurt. But if that has to be . . . '

'Scott! Durrell!' Floyd bellowed.

The two sergeants emerged from the doorway of the officers' quarters, which aligned them physically with Floyd, albeit at several yards distance. But neither the short and stocky Durrell nor the curly-haired, moustached Scott showed anything approaching the grim-faced resolution of the man who had summoned them.

'Let's hear him out, Jack,' Scott said.

'I don't see we got much choice,' Durrell offered.

Floyd expressed contempt for the responses and now looked directly at the Virginian with the little white terrier sitting patiently at his feet. 'Steele?'

'Reckon you've been given good advice, feller.'

The sergeant searched his mind for words to express his feelings. But had to be content with the hackneyed: 'You bastards!' as he whirled and strode back into the command office.

'Yippppeeee!' a man outside the barrack yelled.

'Atta boy, Leon!' another called.

'Where do we start the line, Gemma?' somebody else wanted to know.

'Where's the whisky is more damn important!' This from the trooper in the south east tower.

'Hold it, hold it!' Sibley bellowed, and thrust his carbine high into the air. But he did not have to fire it, the gesture being enough to silence the eager shouts and halt the forward surge. 'Listen, you men! We don't want a friggin' riot with Lone Horn sittin' out there someplace waitin' to hit us! Gemma, get back inside here! Everyone stay calm!'

The sun, the shouting or the threat of being shot down in a crossfire had acted to sober up the woman. Who gasped her shock as she got to her feet, as if only now becoming aware of her nakedness. Then, with a hand cupped between her thighs and an arm across her breasts, she raced for the cover of the hospital.

When she had gone from sight, Sibley grinned and showed the expression to everyone who cared to look at him. 'Take it easy. There's enough for all. Of liquor and that which you've already seen.' Then he became grim-faced again. 'So you men get back to what you was doin' before. While me and the boys get Jack Floyd to see thin's our way.'

Reluctantly, the memory of Gemma Sellers's nude body still fresh in their minds, the soldiers returned to their duty or their rest. While Edward Boucher, his head bandaged aided the women in urging the civilians back into the mess-hall.

Sibley whispered instructions to the troopers who had shared in the hospital orgy and then waited outside while they went through the doorway.

'I hope to God the salesman isn't carrying too many cases,' Colvard growled.

'I could certainly use a drink,' Dunbar muttered.

A pair of boots was tossed out from the hospital and Sibley sat down on the ground to pull them on. As McCoy, having peered thoughtfully at Steele for long moments, started to talk in a rasping whisper.

'Those men are drunk. You saw them. You should get to Floyd before Sibley. He'll know of troopers who want no part of any kind of debauchery. And Scott and Durrell will see reason without carbines aimed at them. It will not take many to ensure that —'

'Steele, no talkin' with the prisoners!' Sibley snapped as he got up from the ground and started across the corner of the compound, the Springfield held two-handed in front of his belly.

Jojo, hearing the tone of voice and sensing animosity, growled softly.

'Some serious talking has to be done, soldier!' Colvard countered grimly. 'There may be a whole tribe of Indians out there just waiting for —'

'Stow it, lieutenant!' Sibley came back with a scowl. 'We'll take care of the friggin' Injuns if they decide to show up! Steele, get back with the rest of the civilians!'

Jojo growled again. But a much more ominous sound was provided by a series of clicks as carbine hammers were cocked.

'Do like the man says!' Moody called from the deep shade of the hospital interior, 'And believe me, I'm still returning the favours you and the shavetail give me!'

'I don't owe anyone any damn thing,' Sibley warned.

'Know the feeling, feller,' the Virginian drawled. And started away from the front of the guardhouse, the terrier trotting faithfully at his heels.

'Damn you to hell, mister!' McCoy snarled after him.

'You like his company that much, Major Friggin' McCoy?' Sibley said, and laughed as he headed for the command office.

'Jojo darling, I was worried about you!' Dora Peachey crooned, stooping down and lifting the dog to her breasts as soon as Steele entered the mess-hall.

The woman had been waiting in the doorway, separate from the rest of the civilians who were sitting or squatting in a group around Edward Boucher. There had obviously been a low-voiced discussion in progress before the Virginian appeared. And Mrs Peachey had apparently been posted at the door to watch for intruders.

'Forget that damn pooch and keep your eyes skinned, Dora!' her husband chided.

'Right,' Boucher rasped, to draw back to himself all the attention which had been diverted towards the newcomer. 'We will take the vote. All those for, show in the usual way.'

A forest of arms were raised into the air, some tentatively, but most eagerly.

'Against.'

Clem Burns, Tom and Mrs Rosenberry. Two other couples, these in their sixties. And George Peachey, who raised both arms and said morosely: 'One for Dora.'

'It's about us leaving the fort, Mr Steele,' the woman hugging the dog explained as the Virginian turned his back on the mess-hall and its occupants to survey the sun-bright compound. 'The younger women and their husbands, they feel

77

that after the Sellers woman has . . . that the soldiers will look elsewhere when they have strong liquor in their blood.'

'I'm so sorry, you folks,' Clarke whined, cleaning the steam from his eyeglasses with a kerchief. 'I should have ditched the stuff aboard my wagon! But I never thought —'

'We have already covered that, sir!' Boucher said sternly. 'You were not to know the situation here and it is the fault of no one in this room!'

'We are going down into the valley, Mr Steele,' Dora Peachey said nervously. 'All of us to the Ivett, Donaldson and Ryker houses. Which are the furthest away now that the Rambach place has gone. And if the savages come, we will hope to talk to them. We have never done them any harm. Only the soldiers from Benedict have done that. Hopefully, they will understand and will leave us in peace.'

'I voted we stay, Dora!' her husband pointed out grimly.

'What's your opinion, mister?' the liquor salesman asked nervously. 'You strike me as the kinda man who's been around? You figure the Injuns will let ordinary folks be?'

'Reckon the Rambachs were ordinary folks,' Steele replied, his gaze fixed upon the open doorway beneath the clock. The time was now almost five and the sun was slanting its rays at an acute angle over the southern section of the west-facing wall of the fort.

'Yeah, but they was new out here. Probably the first time they'd seen Injuns and so they ran scared or put up a fight.'

'Which is what we may have to do, Mr Steele,' the dull-faced Manderson said as soon as Clarke was through. 'Put up a fight. And the more men we got, the better chance we'll have. If Lone Horn and his braves don't listen to reason.'

'I reckon you're thinking too far ahead.'

'Explain yourself, sir,' Boucher demanded.

Steele sighed. As a grinning Sibley and a grim faced Floyd came out of the command office and moved towards the gallows on the centre of the compound. 'I reckon you have a better chance of doing a deal with the Sioux to save your skins – than get out of this place.'

'Nonsense!' Boucher snapped, and strode purposefully through his audience. 'Providing we can make our intentions known while only a handful of the worst element are inebriated, we can convince the decent —'

'All right, hear this!' Sibley yelled from the gallows platform. 'Moody, Hardy, Kupperman, Helm, Adams, you gate sentries! Go haul the liquor wagon in here!'

There was a burst of cheering from several areas of the fort. Which totally masked the groans of despair as the civilians surged towards the doorway and windows of the mess-hall.

Sibley raised his arms, his carbine still clutched in one hand, to demand silence: which he got, except for the thud of booted feet as the detailed men hurried to comply with their order.

'Listen!' the corporal went on, his grin displaced by a frown. 'No man on this post better forget that Lone Horn could be massin' his braves to hit Benedict! So no man better get drunk! Thin's are gonna be much like they was before. With me and Jack Floyd, Charlie Scott and Dave Durrell sayin' what can and can't be done in McCoy's castle!'

'Hell, Leon!' a man on the north-wall walkway complained. 'The liquor and Gemma Sellers just for you and them?'

This triggered a low murmuring of discontent as the gates were swung wide and the work detail went outside.

'Shut up and listen!' Floyd roared.

'No, it ain't gonna be like that!' Sibley snarled into the new, expectant silence. 'What's gonna happen is that we're gonna turn the post hospital into a kinda saloon and cathouse. Where any man who ain't on duty can go get himself a snort or a piece of ass, if he's a mind.'

'Ain't a mind a man needs to —' a trooper yelled excitedly, before his words were drowned out by another cheer and a burst of laughter.

This as Floyd rasped angrily at Sibley, who nodded without enthusiasm and thrust his arms into the air again. Then executed a mocking bow in the direction of the mess-hall.

'Beg your pardon, ladies. For speakin' like I did.'

'But keep this in mind!' Floyd bellowed, and swung his slitted eyes in every direction. 'Anyone who gets too drunk to carry out his duties will be punished!'

'Sergeant!' Edward Boucher called, pushing out through the mess-hall doorway.

'What do you want?' Floyd responded, weary and angry.

'The majority of the civilians wish to leave the post!'

Floyd spat into the dust below the gallows as the liquor wagon was hauled through the gateway, the rattle of bottles sounding louder than the creak of strained timbers. 'You're crazy!'

'We don't think so, sergeant! We feel we can talk with the Indians and —'

'Close those damn gates!' Floyd roared. 'Nobody leaves this post unless ordered to do so!'

Two troopers ran to do his bidding as the liquor-laden wagon was dragged to a halt outside the hospital. Clarke looked at it mournfully – either worried at losing his stock or regretful that he did not get rid of it earlier.

Edward Boucher seemed on the point of challenging Floyd's dictate. But heard his wife call: 'Please, dear. Remember what happened before.'

'Sergeant!' the gaunt-faced lay preacher called as Floyd and Sibley made to go down the steps of the gallows platform.

'I told you, mister, no —'

'If we stay, will you guarantee that we are protected?'

'If Lone Horn hits us, you have to take your chances like the men in uniform! Better chances than you'll have if you're outside when —'

'It is not the Sioux who are our immediate concern, sergeant!' Boucher cut in, and looked pointedly around the fort. 'Particularly those of us with womenfolk to consider!'

There was a hard silence which lasted for several stretched seconds. Then Sibley started to laugh – a harsh sound that was obviously intended to precede a caustic comment on what he thought of the local womenfolk.

But Floyd spoke first. Staring with vicious contempt at the suddenly afraid lay preacher. 'What kind of animals do you think we are, mister? This is the Ninth Cavalry of the United States Army!'

He maintained his fixed stare upon Boucher for a moment more, then continued on his way.

'Sergeant!'

'Don't push him, feller,' Steele offered as Floyd came to a

rigid halt.

'I did not mean to imply that every soldier in this fort is the kind —'

'Best if you just shut your mouth and keep it shut!' Floyd interrupted without turning around. 'And consider yourself demoted, mister. If the civilians wish to bring anythin' to the attention of the military command of Benedict, Steele'll be your spokesman! Understand?'

'But —'

'But me no buts, preacherman!'

Floyd stalked into the command office, yelling for Scott and Durrell to join him. While Sibley headed for the hospital to supervise the unloading of the cases of liquor. And every trooper not on sentry duty looked eagerly at the transfer of unaccustomed supplies.

The post clock struck five. The smell of cooking food – it seemed there was to be beef stew for supper – permeated through the cooling air of early evening.

Edward Boucher, physically sagging under the burden of responsibility he still felt for all the local citizens who looked helplessly at him as he turned, said: 'We can only hope that decency prevails over debauchery. Hope and pray.'

His dispirited eyes met the dark, coldness of Steele's gaze and seemed to express a plea for agreement.

'You heard the man in charge down here, feller,' the Virginian responded flatly. 'I can talk to him. Reckon my line of communication to the higher authority was cut a long time ago.'

'No sinner is beyond redemption. I will mention you in our prayers.'

Boucher came across the threshold and Steele stepped outside.

'Spare one for Jennings and the men in his patrol, feller.'

The anxiety lines in the flesh of the gaunt face suddenly deepened. 'God in heaven. I had forgotten those men!' the lay preacher gasped, and chose to look towards the lowering sun rather than the clock. 'It should not have taken so long to ride to the Rambach place and back.'

'Shouldn't the men in charge be told?' Clarke asked nervously, no longer pompous in his attitude. Still sweating, despite the coolness of evening.

'Sergeant Floyd won't need reminding,' Steele murmured.

'Then why is he allowing drinking and whoring among the men?' Mrs Boucher asked with the usual disdainful sniff that punctuated almost everything she said.

'I reckon, ma'am, because he's seen how easy it is to take control of this post.'

'Which means it's just as easy to lose control, lady,' Clem Burns added, spilling more spittle down his chin as he broke with the group and approached the doorway. Then, as Boucher organised his prayer meeting, the old-timer scanned the fort, noting how many of the men were waiting anxiously for the hospital to open up in a new line of business.

'Let us pray,' the gaunt-faced man said, and began to intone a plea for the safety of all inside the post.

And Burns whispered to Steele: 'Jack Floyd must be countin' on knowin' the boys well enough to figure more will stay sober than get drunk, son.'

'Reckon so.'

'Mighty big gamble. What with them seein' Gemma Sellers ass naked and watchin' all that liquor shifted off the wagon. Guess all them that wanted have been with her before. But not for free. And they never had more than a snort or two over at her place, on account she didn't run no saloon. Needed most of what she had to keep herself goin'.'

'They had the drop on him, feller,' Steele reminded. 'And after that I reckon it was a choice between giving Sibley what he wanted or joining the others in the guardhouse.'

'All right, you guys!' Sibley yelled after climbing up on to the seat of the unloaded wagon. 'Come and get it! Bring your own cups for rye! Guess you all know what you gotta bring to enjoy the other facility we have here at Sibley's Five and a Dollar House of Pleasure!'

They came. Out of the cookhouse, the barracks, the stables, the post store and the officers' quarters. Starting to converge on the hospital the moment Sibley began to yell the invitation. But then the surge came to a halt at the mention of payment.

'Why the charge, Leon?' a man demanded.

'Gemma has to make a livin',' the grinning corporal answered. 'Even if it's just a bare one!'

This raised laughs to counteract the suspicion of anger which was murmuring through the crowd of uniformed figures. And abruptly Sibley was hard-eyed.

'So, a dollar you give the lady. Five cents a shot.'

There was another rumble of discontent.

'All right, I don't mind payin' Gemma,' a trooper allowed. 'But who's gonna get the liquor money?'

'Why Mr Clarke, naturally,' Sibley answered. 'The gent who so kindly provided the supplies.'

'I don't want it,' the man with eye-glasses whined in the mess hall, to reveal that he was more interested in the exchanges out on the compound than the prayer meeting he was attending.

'Don't worry about it, mister,' Clem Burns growled sourly as he and Steele watched the troopers continue their advance upon the hospital, passing under the avaricious gaze of Leon Sibley. 'There's just one man aimin' to make a profit on this deal.'

'What good will money be to anyone if the Sioux catch us unawares?' the suddenly tearful Janet Manderson blurted.

Boucher, at first, angered by the interruptions, grasped the opportunity to make religious capital out of their subject. 'Recall, my brothers and sister, that the meek shall inherit the earth. And that the wages of sin is death! Trust in the Lord our God!'

There were scuffles among the sixty or so men anxious to get into the hospital. Then irate shouts as Sibley leapt down from the wagon seat to join Moody, Kupperman and two other troopers who sought to bring some kind of order to the crowd.

'Lived more than seventy years and I've always said it, mister,' Burns muttered bitterly. 'Of all the seven deadly sins, them that causes the most trouble are gluttony and lust.'

'Deadly could be right, feller,' Steele answered flatly. 'If the Sioux show up after too many pigs have bought a poke.'

Chapter Nine

Steele was in the command office, trying to convince Sergeant Floyd that he should send out a second patrol to check the whereabouts of the first, when Janet Manderson screamed her terror.

It was seven-thirty and the Virginian had been in the spartanly furnished, once neat and clean but now disarrayed office for more than twenty minutes. With Floyd, Scott and Durrell, all of them eating beef stew and then drinking coffee: the trio of noncoms agreeing with Steele's evenly-voiced assessment of the dangers of the situation but resolutely refusing to do anything about what was happening. Yet.

Or rather, Jack Floyd constantly growled: 'Yeah, Steele, we know. But we'll protect anythin' that needs protectin' when the time comes,' and the other two sergeants always nodded that they shared this view.

'Damn civilians!' the man with iron-grey hair and narrowed eyes snarled, knocking his chair over backwards as he rose fast at the sound of the scream. Then yelled for Scott and Durrell to clear out of his way as he rounded the side of the desk and took long strides to the window.

Steele was already there, standing against the wall as he finished his coffee, and had simply to turn around and take a step to the side to get a view of the compound.

Full night was clamped over the Dakotas now, but the moon

was high and large and bright: its glow supplemented by several wedges of lamplight from windows. Little came from the command office for the lamp on the desk emitted just a pale-yellow glimmer from a turned-down wick. So that the four men who gazed from the window were able to see clearly the scene in front of the mess-hall without having to peer through their own reflections on the glass.

'Seems like you have to protect the good name of the Ninth Cavalry, sergeant,' Steele said.

The young and pretty Mrs Manderson was sprawled face down on the compound six feet away from the open doorway of the mess-hall. Had apparently fallen as she was dragged outside by the overweight Trooper Kupperman, who now stooped, swaying drunkenly, to get a grip on one of the woman's wrists.

Between her and the mess-hall stood the redhaired Trooper Hardy and the soldier named Adams who was probably the shortest man on the post for he stood no taller than five feet. Both of them had cocked Colts in their wavering hands, aimed through the doorway.

When the terrified woman screamed again, as Kupperman got a firm grip on her and straightened, hauling her half to her feet, the sound was almost lost amid a burst of noise from the men grouped in front of the hospital and around the unloaded liquor wagon. Cheers, shouts of encouragement for the fat trooper and the venting of harsh laughter.

The three noncoms were on their way out of the command office by then – snatching up carbines from where the guns leaned against the front of the desk as they headed for the door.

Steele remained where he was, merely set down his cup on the window sill and picked up and cocked the Colt Hartford. As Jojo, with a bark of delight, streaked in through the open door from the hallway where the Virginian had made him wait.

The Virginian's dark eyes raked over every section of the fort which was visible from the window. And saw that the sentries on the walkways and in the towers at either end of the south wall had turned to see what was causing the noise.

And that a small group of sober troopers had spilled from the barrack. Ten of them, looking scared. As opposed to the more than forty – many with cups of liquor in their fists – who jostled for a better view in front of the hospital.

'Leave her alone! Leave my wife be!'

'Freeze, or I'll kill you!'

Manderson shrieking in panic and Hardy responding in a tone that demanded the threat be taken seriously. The latter silencing the screams and shouts from inside the mess-hall. And subduing the noise of the men out in front of the hospital.

Kupperman fastened a grip on Janet Manderson's other wrist and, as the woman began to be wracked by sobs, lifted her up on to her knees. Which brought her waxen, tear-run face on a level with his crotch. With a grin spread across his drink-sodden, fleshy features, the trooper arched his back to press the base of his bulging belly against the face of Mrs Manderson. And yelled:

'That's right, my little darlin'! You learn fast! Already you got the idea.'

'Fire!' Floyd roared.

And a carbine cracked. Cutting across the shrieking words of Kupperman. Sending a bullet over the top of the gallows platform to bite deep into the timber of a gate. Silencing every sound in Fort Benedict, except for the exhausted sobs of the humiliated woman, for a period of three stretched seconds.

Then Kupperman released her and threw himself to the side, pressing his bulky body to the ground. Mrs Manderson flopped forward, hit her chin hard on the fat trooper's boot heel and lay still and quiet in unconsciousness.

Hardy and Adams whirled to look and aim at the front of the command office.

Floyd ordered: 'Put up them guns, you men.'

As, with a groan of utter despair, the dull-faced Manderson lurched from the mess-hall doorway, barged aside the two troopers and hurled himself down into a crouch beside his inert wife.

'Hell, Jack!' Leon Sibley complained, his voice slurred by alcohol, as he elbowed his way clear of the press of men around the wagon. 'Gemma's passed out cold and there ain't half the men got to lay her yet!'

As the corporal spoke, the sergeant who fired the shot pushed another bullet into the breech of the Springfield.

'Charlie, Dave?' Sibley implored.

While Kupperman got unsteadily to his feet and backed away from the hatred he saw on Menderson's face after the civilian had turned his wife over on to her back and cradled her head on his kneeling legs.

'Shit, Leon!' a man in the crowd behind Sibley called. 'We got 'em outnumbered!'

He pushed to the front, showing the Colt he had drawn. It was the forty-year-old Helm who had a scar on his right cheek and the lobe missing from his right ear. Two other troopers emerged from the group to flank him, both with revolvers in their fists. Hardy and Adams had not complied with Floyd's order. There was scuffling in the group out front of the hospital as more liquor brave troopers struggled to draw Colts.

The handful of men who had emerged from the barrack were only half-dressed and were not armed. No sentry visible on the walkways showed any inclination to take part in what was happening below.

Until Steele drew mass attention to himself. By pushing the muzzle of the Colt Hartford hard against the window: causing the pane to shatter and spew shards noisily on the ground beneath where he stood. Aiming at nothing but obviously aligned with Floyd.

Then Corporal Jordan shouted down from his vantage point behind the Gatling gun in the moon shadow of the north-west tower.

'I got them in my sights, Jack!'

'Frig it!' Sibley snarled.

'Just say the word, Leon,' Helm invited.

Boot leather scraped on floorboards and the light from the mess-hall doorway was partially blocked by the tall form of Tom Rosenberry and the much shorter one of the ugly Stan Ivett. Both men had Winchester rifles against their shoulders, aimed at the backs of Hardy and Adams.

87

'Frig it!' Sibley repeated, with even more force behind the words.

And silence, hard and tense, clamped down over the fort for stretched seconds. Until it was broken by a voice from above the gateway.

'Sergeant Floyd! Leon! Whichever of you is the big man now! Riders comin' in on the trail!'

'What kind? How many?' This from Floyd as he strode away from the command office doorway, Springfield sloped diagonally across his belly and chest. Confidence and authority in the way he held himself and the measured length of his strides.

'Eight or ten horses, maybe! But I only see two men in the saddles! White men, looks like! Yeah. Army, sergeant! Way the moonlight shines on their buttons!'

'Keep them covered all the way, soldier!' Floyd was beyond the gallows as he gave this order. And lowered his voice without detracting from the hardness in his tone as he snapped. 'Hardy, Adams, prepare to open the gates on my order! Manderson, get your wife back in the mess-hall!'

'But —'

'But me no buts, mister! Move your ass and that woman out of here!'

'Here, I'll give you a hand, son,' Clem Burns offered, coming out of the mess-hall doorway and knocking aside the two men with Winchesters.

Sibley spoke a fast order to the men with drawn Colts at his side and they slid the revolvers back into the holsters. Then the corporal – like everyone else who had been drinking, sobered by the news of advancing riders – broke into a run to climb the ladder to the walkway immediately behind Floyd.

Jojo whined and Steele canted the Colt Hartford to his shoulder and stooped to caress the head of the dog before he left the command office to move out on to the compound.

With one period of tension eased, another started to build. Noncoms and troopers who had previously divided into opposing factions were abruptly of one mind as they advanced on the gate facing side of the gallows. Steele, the terrier again

88

at his heels, moved in front of the officers' mess to the barred window of the guardhouse. The faces of McCoy, Colvard, Dunbar and Starling showed pale on the other side of the bars. With no chance of seeing what was about to happen, the two troopers who shared the cell continued to sit on one of the cots.

'God, that was close,' the sad-eyed Starling rasped.

'Two men with a bunch of riderless horses,' McCoy said ominously. 'Pickets bringing in what's left of Jennings's patrol.'

'Good bet,' Steele allowed.

Words were shouted up to the walkway from outside the fort. They did not carry as far as the opposite side of the compound.

'Open the gates, soldiers!' Floyd yelled down.

As Hardy and Adams obeyed the command, all attention except that of Steele was directed towards the entrance of Benedict.

During his earlier visit with the prisoners, he had seen through the wall of bars which formed one side of the cell, most of the other section of the guardhouse. Just a chair and a desk with a bulletin board on the wall behind. When he entered this area now, and closed the door behind him, the only light in the place came through the cell window. Just enough, with the officers blocking most of it, for him to find his way to the desk.

'Top-left-hand drawer, sir,' Lieutenant Colvard supplied. 'If you're looking for the keys.'

Steele glanced up as he opened the specified drawer. And saw in silhouette the forms of the lieutenant and two troopers standing against the wall of bars.

'Good man,' McCoy said.

'There's a condition,' the Virginian countered as he lifted from the drawer an iron ring with three keys on it.

'Hurry up, man! While we still have the diversion.'

'Recommend you listen to what Mr Steele has in mind, major,' Colvard advised.

'Go ahead, sir,' Starling urged.

'Floyd hasn't put a foot wrong so far but —'

'Not a foot wrong —' McCoy started.

'Shut up, major!' Colvard cut in.

'Why —'

'Not now, sir,' Starling implored.

'Or I'll damn well shut you up!' Dunbar added.

The deposed commanding officer of Fort Benedict made a gagging sound: like that of a man drowning in his own vomit.

'But,' Steele continued, 'I don't reckon he can handle any more pressures.'

'Like us storming out of here and trying to pull rank, uh?' Dunbar suggested.

'Right, feller.'

'Try is right,' Colvard added. 'With just these two men and Steele to back us, we wouldn't last —'

'Don't include me, lieutenant,' Steele corrected. 'I just reckon to be on the side with the most survivors, which I aim to include me.'

'Get to the point, man!' McCoy demanded, almost composed again.

'I think the same way as you do about what is coming in through the gates, major. And from my experience with Indians, they don't send messages for the hell of it.'

'A taste of what they plan for the rest of us,' McCoy agreed, nodding.

Dunbar groaned. 'How can he get to the point if you keep —'

'Stow it, all of you!' Colvard snapped irritably.

Steele sighed. 'I'm going to unlock the cell door now. Because I may not get the chance later and maybe no one else will think of it. But you fellers will only come out if and when the Sioux hit the fort. If you're seen to be free before then, it could be Floyd will lose what support he has. And lose control.'

'Makes sense, sir,' Colvard said.

And Starling and Dunbar made noises of agreement.

Steele unlocked the door with the second key he tried, returned the bunch to the desk and went out on to the compound again. Jojo was waiting for him, as patient as ever. There was a new, almost complete silence: tense in the cool night air again. Disturbed by the clop of many sets of slow-moving hooves.

'We're much obliged to you, Mr Steele,' Starling said through the barred window. 'It doesn't bear thinking about, what would happen to us if the Sioux took Benedict and found us locked in this place.'

'I don't think it was that caused him to give us an escape chance,' McCoy added, now fully in control of himself. 'Sergeant Floyd's a fine soldier and an excellent non-commissioned officer. Who might just be able to defend Fort Benedict against a full attack by Sioux. But in this kind of situation, any commander needs as many able-bodied men as he can muster.'

'Right, major,' the Virginian confirmed as he headed across the compound as the two pickets who had been positioned at the head of the Barton River Valley rode through the gateway. Behind them, strung out almost to the gap in the defensive half-circle where the liquor wagon had been removed, was a line of eight horses roped together.

Not riderless, as had been reported at first. But it was a mistake easy to make over a distance. For the riders were not astride the horses. Instead, they were slumped over the saddles. What was left of them, anyway.

The elderly Lieutenant Jennings, a corporal and the six troopers who had ridden by Steele in the early morning – the officer demanding silence in the column, his men eager to show their dislike for Steele.

Perhaps they had all been shot dead in ambush before the knives and tomahawks were used on their flesh. The return of the corpses delayed until after dark because the Sioux considered it was more effective to induce horror and terror at night than in bright sunlight.

Or maybe some or all of the cavalrymen had been captured alive. And it had taken an entire slow day to put them to brutal death. The braves – or even the squaws – cutting off living flesh a piece at a time. Fingers and toes, noses and genitals, slices of belly and buttocks, then the ears and eyes. The scalps of close-cropped hair, of course. Somewhere in the evil process, the men's tongues had been removed. A final

91

skull cleaving blow with a tomahawk. Or maybe the single bullet blasted into the heart of each man was the last violation of his body. As part of the ritual, or to end mercifully his living nightmare of unimaginable agony.

The mutilated corpses, naked and run with dark, unmoving rivers of congealed blood, were in some cases lashed face down over the saddles and in others bent backwards across them. So that, as the sick-looking troopers led the string of horses into the fort, those who watched in stunned silence were able to see the full extent of the Sioux's brutality towards the men.

The mounts to which the corpses were lashed had coats crusted with the dried lather, dust-stained, of old sweat.

One of the troopers who had brought in the bodies was the thin, blond-haired Cass. He seemed less affected by the line or horror strung out behind him than the older, taller, fatter man who had shared the Barton River Valley sentry duty with him. Fractionally.

It was he who called a halt when the last of the exhausted horses was inside the fort, and who spoke to Floyd and Sibley when the two noncoms had reached the ground and moved to the head of the column.

'Me and Williams seen the horses comin' hell for leather along the river, sarge.' When Steele heard the trooper speak much earlier in the day, his voice had sounded young and vibrant: slightly shrill with excitement as he referred to the willing Gemma Sellers. His words were now hoarse and he sounded older than Clem Burns. 'Injuns roped them together and put burrs under the saddles. But they was easy to stop. Near on their knees from runnin'. When we saw what the bastards done to the men, we puked. Them bastards are warnin' us, sarge. Ain't that what this is all about? The friggin' butchers figure to do this to all of —'

'Dismount, Cass!' Floyd barked, and his tone was almost as thick as that of the trooper. 'You, too, Williams! Leon, see these men get a drink! Close them damn gates! Kupperman! You, you, you, you!' He stabbed a finger at four men in the front rank of the shocked, watching group of troopers. 'Take the horses to the stables! Cut the bodies loose and wrap them in blankets! Sergeant Scott, detail a burial squad! Just the one hole out back of the fort! Don't waste no time! Hardy, Girling – go replace Cass and Williams at the head of the valley! You men on the walls keep your eyes skinned!'

'Hey, Leon!' the squint-eyed Hardy complained in a whining tone. 'Jack's pickin' us for the shit duties just because we —'

'Do like you're told!' Sibley snapped at the resentful trooper. 'Party's over!' He raked his eyes, still partially glazed by the shock of looking at the mutilated dead, across the faces of all the troopers on the compound. 'For everybody!'

The men began to disperse, just a few of them disgruntled. Most of them afraid. The troopers detailed for specific duties moved to complete them. On his way back to the command office, Floyd paused beside where Steele stood, the white terrier seated at his heels.

'With the patrol so long gone, I knew somethin' like this had happened,' the sergeant said, his voice sounding as weary as his face looked. 'As Indians go, Lone Horn ain't a bad guy. Except when his back's up. And Major Friggin' McCoy killin' a whole bunch of his braves was bound to put the chief's back up right high. No point in riskin' another patrol out beyond the picket line. Lookin' for a heap of bodies.'

Steele nodded. 'Apart from your bad timing of the mutiny, feller, you've been right all along the line.'

Floyd swilled some saliva around in his mouth and spat it at the lowest step of the gallows platform. 'If I hadn't started it then, Leon Sibley would've. Which would've got the men behind him without need of hard liquor and the Sellers whore to make him popular.' He looked grimly up at the gallows frame. 'And Major Friggin' McCoy would be strung up. Maybe the rest of the officers would be dead as well.'

'You have a reason for telling me all this, sergeant?'

The tall noncom with the slitted blue eyes and too-short mouth sighed. 'Sometimes a man needs to talk. Guess right now all I really want to say is thanks – for backin' me when the situation looked like it was gettin' outta hand.'

The Virginian nodded his acknowledgement. 'Always like to be on the winning side. Best when it's the one with right on it, too.'

'Just hope the court-martial judges see it that way, Mr Steele,' Floyd said with an embittered smile.

'No point in worrying about something that might never happen,' Steele replied.

'It'll happen, mister,' Floyd muttered, every trace of the wry humour gone from his features. 'Don't *you* worry about that. Ain't no way the army's gonna just pat me on the fanny and tell me —'

'I was talking,' the Virginian said, looking out of the gates which had been opened to allow through the burial detail and their gristly burdens, 'about your future.'

Chapter Ten

At midnight Fort Benedict was silent, save for the snores and heavy breathing of deeply sleeping men and women and the occasional snort of a restless horse. Up on the walkways and in the towers, the newly posted reliefs for the former sentries stood tensely at their positions. Peering intently out over the moonlit terrain, hoping and praying that they would not see any signal of impending danger from the forward pickets.

Steele was not asleep, although he gave the impression he was as he lay sprawled out on his back on and under blankets close to the mess-hall doorway. His hat was over his face and the Colt Hartford lay at his side, hidden by the covering blanket. Earlier he had slept, lulled by the regular thud of spades biting into the ground out back of the fort. But the noise made by the changeover of guards had disturbed him and after that he found it impossible to doze off again.

So he lay awake, recalling previous Indian troubles that had involved him: and other occasions when he had sought the shelter of an army post for one reason or another. The Apaches down in Sonora when the Colt Hartford was stolen from him. Later, the Comanches in Texas. More Apaches in the Mexican Baja when he was charged with returning the young Jimmy Dexter to his California home. Fort Pepper with Mrs Lucifer and her strange band of travelling whores. Fort Baxter where an officer who hated Indians as much as McCoy apparently did, stirred up trouble with the Shoshonis. As far back as the war, where there had been no Indians. But many army posts where Steele, as a soldier, had to abide by the rules and regulations laid down by the various commanding officers.

Here, tonight, he wore no uniform and was at the fort from choice. True, once inside, Floyd insisted that the civilians remain. But to a man like the Virginian, there would be little difficulty in escaping the stockade if he elected to take that course. The Sioux? A lone man on foot at night would have a far better chance of evading them than a mounted patrol of eight cavalrymen in broad daylight.

A far greater chance of survival, too, than if he was one of the defenders left alive after a successful Indian attack.

But he had made his choice and thus felt committed to staying right where he was. Even though he was concerned by the attitude of most of the troopers and noncoms as they looked upon the gruesome end results of Sioux vengeance.

The large majority of men on the post were in their early twenties – too young to have seen active duty in the War Between the States and doubtless lacking in experience of Indian fighting. Whereas men like Captain Starling, Lieutenant Dunbar and Trooper Helm in the forty-to-fifty age group could well have fought many battles against various enemies but they now gave the impression of being soft and unfit.

Apart from Manderson and perhaps a half-dozen home-steaders, the civilian men were for the most part in the middle-to-old age group. And all of them, except for the oldest of all – Clem Burns – would be as much concerned for the safety of their women as for their own survival in any kind of pitched battle.

Jack Floyd would keep constantly on top of the situation, provided he did not crack under the strain. But the effects of pressure were already starting to show.

Major McCoy was probably the best man available to command the defence of Benedict – were he in charge of a troop who had had no time to come to detest him.

Lieutenant Michael Colvard also had leadership capabilities – unless he failed to learn quickly that West Point theory did not always prepare a man for the harsh practice of Indian fighting.

Steele himself? He grimaced into the pitch-black underside of his hat. Never, unless there was a strong possibility of good material reward. Or his own life depended upon others surviving. Under any other circumstances, he did not want that kind of responsibility.

So why was he here?

The grimace was replaced by a look of total impassiveness in the secret darkness beneath his hat as he admitted the answer to himself. And fisted his gloved hand tightly around the frame of the Colt Hartford.

It had been a long time since he last killed anybody.

'Sergeant! Sergeant Floyd! They're comin', sarge!'

The excited and frightened shouting triggered a cacophony of other raised voices all around the fort. In the mess-hall, too, as those who came awake sluggishly demanded of the light sleepers to know what was happening.

As on the other occasions when a period of peace and quiet in Benedict was shattered by words which presaged violence, men and women spilled from doorways or pressed their faces to windows.

Steele, the immensely tall Tom Rosenberry and the ugly Stan Ivett stood in a firm line on the mess-hall threshold: preventing the civilians from encroaching more than a few inches on to the compound. Where the troopers waited, holstered Colts on their hips and Springfield carbines in their hands, watching as Floyd ran towards the gate – yelling for silence.

'The pickets from the head of the valley, sarge!' the trooper above the gates called down as all other voices were stilled and galloping hooves could be heard out on the trail. 'And it looks like . . . yeah, sarge! A red glow and smoke! The bastards are settin' fire to the settlers' places!'

'Easy, soldier!' Floyd urged. 'Everyone take it easy! Keep watch in every direction!'

He went to the gates and opened one of them. Just wide enough for the scar-faced Helm and the broad-nosed, almost chinless Girling to ride through. The two troopers entered the post at a full gallop and brought their mounts to a rearing, dust-billowing halt.

7   97

'Down the valley, Jack!' Girling yelled as he leapt from his saddle. 'The whole friggin' Sioux nation looks like. Ridin' down the valley and tossin' torches at every buildin' they come to!'

Floyd directed a contemptuous look at the panting, sweating man and shifted his gaze to the slightly less agitated Helm. 'How many? Reasonable estimate, soldier?'

'Figure at least two hundred,' the trooper answered. 'Maybe as many as three. They comin' at a steady canter. Hard to see exactly how many over that distance. With them all on the move. And lots of them hidden by smoke most of the time.'

Silence, with every eye except those of the guards on the wall directed towards the abruptly calm and pensive Floyd.

'We'll say close to three,' he said, speaking aloud his thoughts. Became suddenly aware that this was what he had done and raised his voice. 'Close to three hundred is as many as Lone Horn could raise! All of them headin' for us from the same direction! Aimin' to scare the crap out of us with that many Injuns all in one group! Turn the screws on whatever he figured to do to us with the Rambach raid and what he done to Lieutenant Jennin's and the boys! Typical of old Lone Horn! But don't let the bastards get to you!'

He raked his slit-eyed stare around the fort.

'We got the beatin' of them! Lone Horn's got the numbers, but we got the fire-power! Remember that!'

Another all-encompassing survey of the buildings and men on three sides of where he stood.

'All right! Sibley, Scott, Durrell! We talked about what we was gonna do! Detail your men and do it! Helm, Girling! mount up again and go bring in the flank and rear pickets!'

As his orders were put into effect, Floyd began to climb the closest ladder to the south-wall walkway. At the top he looked down on to and across the compound: beckoned to Steele that the Virginian should come and join him.

'Everyone stay inside,' Steele rasped across a rising volume of talk from the civilians who were crowding himself and Rosenberry and Ivett. 'The men with guns check them over. I'll be back.'

As he crossed the compound, he shot a glance between the

moving forms of cavalrymen hurrying to comply with commands shouted by the noncoms designated by Floyd. And he saw the pale blurs of faces behind the bars in the guardhouse window. But there was no way in which he could send a tacit message through the milling throng of soldiers over such a distance. So he had to rely on the common sense of the prisoners to realise that it was not yet time for their break for freedom.

When he reached the top of the ladder and crossed to stand beside Floyd, the flames of many raging fires were painting a vast domelike glow of redness over the sky above the southern horizon. The coloration darkened from time to time by billowing clouds of black smoke.

Immediately below where they stood the gates of the fort were open and men were running through. A squad towards the Sellers's house where an artillery piece was concealed in the stable. Three other squads went to the trio of twelve-pounders positioned behind the half-circle of wagons.

More troopers were manhandling the empty liquor wagon out of the gateway, ready to plug the gap in the defensive arc of vehicles as soon as all the forward pickets were back at the post.

Inside the fort, the majority of troopers filed slowly into the magazine, emerged with a supply of shells for their carbines and doubled across to ladders – climbed them to take up predetermined positions on the walkways.

Sibley was in command of the north wall, Scott the east and Durrell the west. On the south wall, Floyd ignored all the activity around and below him to keep a pair of field-glasses trained on the ridge over which he expected the Sioux to appear.

A sound rang out, sharp and clear from the body of noise made by those preparing to defend Fort Benedict from Indian attack. A sharp bark as Jojo raced from the open doorway of the mess-hall. The little white terrier streaked across the busy compound, came to a sudden halt at the foot of the ladder Steele had climbed and sat down. And remained there, head cocked to one side, gazing up dolefully to where he expected the Virginian to reappear.

'You were in the army once, weren't you Steele?' Floyd asked without relaxing his vigil on the ridge.

'Right, feller.'

'The war?'

'Right again.'

'Officer, I bet.'

'Three in a row.'

'So you don't like what I've done to McCoy and the others.'

'Me being an officer a lot of years ago has nothing to do with my feelings about that.'

'Guess it don't matter, anyway – how you feel about anythin' except stayin' alive. What I want you to do is take command of the civilians. Most of them are able-bodied and a lot of them got guns. Handguns mostly. But we got a few surplus carbines in the magazine. Issue them to the men you think'll do most good with them. And there's gonna be some more Springfields lyin' around after the Sioux have hit us. You know what I mean?'

'Dead men kill no Indians, feller.'

'You'll do it?'

'I'll try. But a man in uniform would be better. I've got no authority over the settlers.'

Floyd spat between his forearms, the field-glasses still held to his eyes. The globule arced out over the sharpened tops of the trunks forming the wall and down to the hard-packed dirt below. 'I just given you the authority, mister. And you got my say-so to shoot any man – or woman – who don't follow your orders.'

Steele was on the point of refusing the sergeant's request, but forced himself to turn away and move along the creaking boards to the head of the ladder.

'Mister!' Floyd called and even now did not shift his concentrated attention away from the ridge in the south. 'Keep the civilians in reserve. Ain't their trade – defendin' army property from hostiles. But they got a right to defend themselves. Better chance of doin' that if a man like you shows them how.'

The Virginian climbed to the foot of the ladder and moved across the compound, the small dog trotting at his heels.

The gates were closed now and all the men were in their

100

assigned positions – staring tensely towards the ridge, the line of which was sharply inscribed against the fierce red glow of countless raging fires in the valley beyond.

The firm closing of the gates served to emphasise the feeling of being trapped which Steele had started to experience from the moment he turned away from Sergeant Floyd. Ensnared by responsibility for the welfare and even lives of other people. Even worse, other people to whom he owed nothing.

Which went totally against the grain of everything he had become since the final violent postscript to a long, hard war during which it was his sworn duty to lead others considered less able than himself.

And yet he had agreed, with only a token and weak objection, to Floyd's request that he set aside his philosophy of self-interest first and last to accept accountability for a motley group of untrained and untried men and women for whom he felt no liability.

But there was a good reason for the decision he took and he acknowledged this with a short sigh which whistled through clenched teeth as he halted outside the mess-hall doorway and turned to rake his cold gaze around the walkways lined with men.

Men who were unwashed and stubbled, some of them attired in dishevelled uniforms, many doubtless suffering the nagging headaches and sour tastes of over-indulgence in liquor. Their appearance vastly different from that which Major McCoy had demanded when he was in command of the post.

But in this situation, the turn-out of the troopers and non-coms was unimportant, except that it was a symptom of their ability or lack of it to meet the Sioux threat. And how they responded to the impending attack by Lone Horn and his braves would depend upon the quality of leadership. Without firm and controlled command the men were likely to become a panicked and undisciplined mob. And, as Steele had reflected earlier, Jack Floyd was the only man on the post capable of such command – providing he did not crack under the strain.

A refusal by the Virginian – obviously the only man Floyd thought able to take charge of the civilians – could well have been the critical blow to shatter the nervy noncom's already seriously undermined self-confidence. And with a man like Sibley giving the orders . . .

So, with the sigh, Steele concluded that, faced with a massed attack by hostile Sioux it was very much in his own self-interest to do as Floyd asked.

'Mr Steele!'

Gemma Sellers called his name in a harsh whisper from the darkened doorway of the hospital. Then emerged on to the moon-shadowed compound and came towards him as he looked at her. The white dress was creased and streaked with dirt. Her face was puffy, and pale except for dark segments beneath her bloodshot eyes. Her long red hair hung straight and lifeless. She was unsteady on her bare feet. She looked ill and miserable and when she got close enough Steele could smell on her flesh her own and the sweat of countless men.

'You want something, ma'am?' he asked.

'It's cold and lonely in there.' She waved a hand carelessly in the direction of the building she had just left. 'Do you think they'll allow me to come back in —'

'We want no harlots with us!' Edward Boucher snarled.

'Step inside,' Steele invited.

The tall and gaunt lay preacher was flanked on the threshold of the mess-hall by the even taller Tom Rosenberry and the elderly Clem Burns. Both these men stepped back. But not far, for a great many of the civilians had advanced on the doorway when Steele was seen to be returning from his talk with Floyd.

'I do not know what that mutinous sergeant said to you, sir!' Boucher rasped. 'But I still consider myself the guardian of the morals of these —'

'Floyd said I should shoot anyone who doesn't do what I tell them,' the Virginian cut in evenly.

Gasps rippled through the press of people in back of where Boucher stood – rigid with indignation, his complexion almost as white as the dressing on his head wound.

Jojo sensed the emnity directed towards Steele and vented a long, low-keyed growl.

'Back up and let the lady inside, feller.'

102

'No! You would not dare to shoot an unarmed man who preaches the word of God!'

Boucher splayed his feet and folded his arms across his chest.

'Edward!' his wife called from the rear of the crowd. And on this occasion she did not finish with her usual sniff.

'You're right,' Steele said as he moved towards the doorway, rifle canted to his left shoulder, face impassive under the power of the taller man's challenging scowl. 'Could bring down a Sioux brave with the bullet I'd waste on you.'

The Virginian sensed scorn emanating from the mess-hall: that he had apparently backed down before the defiance of Boucher. Gemma Sellers had no energy to generate such a powerful emotion. She simply groaned and started to turn wearily away. But snapped her head around as she heard an explosion of shocked gasps and cries. These sounds of surprise and alarm triggered by a series of sudden moves from Steele.

First, as he got close to Boucher, the Virginian raised his right gloved hand to his neck, fisted it around one weighted corner of his kerchief and pulled it free. In a wrist-twisting action that wrenched the scarf from around his own neck and sent it flying over the taller man's shoulder.

Boucher tried to take a backward step, the movement instinctive. But the free-swinging weighted corner of the silken kerchief curved around the back of his neck and over his other shoulder.

Steele had let the Colt Hartford drop to the ground by then. And brought up his right hand to grasp the kerchief. Then he crossed his forearms and interlocked the crook of his right elbow with that of the right.

Thus, in the second since he began the attack, he had the taller man trapped in a stranglehold. And he pulled the two corners of the kerchief taut enough to constrict the windpipe of the lay preacher.

Boucher had managed to force out a partial cry of terror before he was silenced. Then he raised his hands, fingers clawed, to try to hook them under the fabric. But it was too fine and too tightly applied: sunk into even the sparse flesh of his throat. And he dropped his hands, defeated. Then fell hard down on to his knees when Steele lowered his arms.

'This way, nothing gets wasted,' the Virginian said flatly when he was in a position to look down into the purple-tinged, bulging-eyed face of Boucher. 'Except your life.'

'Don't!' Mrs Boucher pleaded as she broke clear of the front of the crowd. 'Please don't kill him.'

'Shut up, ma'am,' Steele said in the same tone of voice, and eased up a little. So that the man kneeling before him was able to expel stale air and suck in fresh – with noisy difficulty. 'Listen, Mr Boucher. If you want to take care of the souls of these people, that's between you and them. I don't happen to think that any of them will go to hell just because a part-time whore spends some time in a room with them.'

'Opposite, seems to me,' Clem Burns growled. 'Show they got christian charity.'

'Yes, yes, she can come in!' Mrs Boucher blurted. 'Please, release —'

Her husband made a gurgling sound and when words failed to emerge, injected a plea into his eyes.

'Listen just awhile longer, feller,' Steele insisted. 'I'm going to let you go and then I'm going to tell everyone here what they have to do in the defence of this fort. Which means what we all have to do to save our own skins. Anyone doesn't do what he or she is told will be siding with the Sioux. And we're here to see that the Sioux get beaten.'

He released his grip on one corner of the scarf and stepped back, pulling the fabric clear of Boucher's neck and draping it around his own. By the time he had picked up the rifle, Mrs Boucher had flung herself down beside her kneeling husband and was embracing him. As he massaged the circle of inflamed flesh on his throat.

There was still some scorn emanating from within the mess-hall. And some fear. Also something akin to respect. Impossible to tell in what proportions.

'After you, ma'am,' Steele said to Gemma Sellers, and ushered her with his free hand towards the doorway.

'Thanks,' the woman croaked. 'You're very kind, Mr Steele.'

'He's mean and vicious, that is what he is!' Mrs Boucher

countered, as her husband tried, ineffectual through weakness, to silence her. 'As hard as his name.'

'Pleasure was all mine,' the Virginian said to Gemma Sellers with a brief, tight smile. As he recalled his conclusion about the reason he elected to remain at Fort Benedict. 'In my line of work I guess a man has to be hard as steel. Happy to find out I haven't got rusty.'

Chapter Eleven

The Sioux rode their ponies up on to the ridge at sunrise.

All through the tension-filled night there were whispered exchanges among both the uniformed men and the civilian population of the post that Lone Horn would time his attack at just after daybreak. But just as many defenders of Fort Benedict maintained that the elderly Indian chief would elect to use the cover of darkness. And no one was sufficiently convinced by the daybreak theory to relax his vigil. So no one slept.

But if anyone felt the draining effects of fatigue as the sun inched above the eastern horizon they were terrifyingly wide-awake a few moments later.

The braves appeared on the southern ridge in ranks of three, the line of mounts and riders stretching perhaps a hundred yards from east to west. At the very centre of the front row was the warrior who Jack Floyd identified as Lone Horn: muttering the name through unmoving lips as he trained the field glasses on the chief. Speaking aloud a thought rather than to inform the Virginian who stood beside him on the walkway above the gate.

The chief wore a double-tailed war bonnet of eagle feathers, decorated leggings and a breechclout. Around his neck was a bear-claw necklace. There was no paint on his naked torso. Flanking him, two on each side, were his sub-chiefs who wore less ornate war bonnets and decorated war shirts and leggings. Unlike Lone Horn, these Indians had paint on their faces.

All the braves wore some feathers in their headbands and all had on leggings. Some had adopted vests, some shirts and a number were bare to the waist. Only the sub-chiefs carried lances. A few of the braves had bows across their backs. The majority carried rifles or carbines. Knives, tomahawks and revolvers hung from weapon belts.

Steele saw the Indians in detail through the field-glasses which Jack Floyd thrust absently into his hands as the non-com completed his own survey and yelled to his men:

'All right, you seen them! Don't no one get trigger happy until he's sure they're in range! You men on the cannons, hold your fire until I give the word!'

'I reckon they want to bargain, feller,' Steele said. And handed the glasses back to Floyd.

The sergeant took them, but did not need to use them in order to see that one of the sub-chiefs and three braves had heeled their ponies out of the line. To gallop the animals towards the fort. A piece of white fabric flew in the slipstream from the point of the sub-chief's lance.

'Hey, Jack!' Corporal Jordan yelled from his post behind the south-east Gatling gun. 'They'll spot our artillery pieces.'

'Tricky bastards!' Arnie Moody snarled from his walkway position. And cocked his Springfield.

'No shootin'!' Floyd ordered, and focused the field-glasses on the fast-riding group of Sioux. Then muttered as he lowered them: 'Crazy Pony and well-named.'

'How well do you know the local Sioux?' Steele asked.

'Well enough not to trust any of them further than I can spit into a winter norther!' the army sergeant answered in a growl. 'And to know that's the way they feel about us as well.'

'But you're going to listen?'

Floyd showed brief anger. 'I ain't never shot at nobody under a flag of truce, mister.'

'What's happenin' out there?' Clem Burns yelled, shrill and nervous, from the doorway of the mess-hall.

Floyd opened his mouth to shout an angry retort, but Steele beat him to the words.

'Four men coming in to talk.'

'Why don't you print up a newsheet and pass it around, Steele?' the sergeant growled.

'You wanted me because I was an army officer, feller,' the Virginian answered flatly. 'Always found my troop fought better when they knew what was going on.'

Floyd nodded and allowed, grudgingly: 'There ain't too many of you around, mister.'

'Reckon a lot of people are glad I'm just one of a kind,' Steele answered.

Like the rest of the men upon the south wall walkway, the noncom and the civilian did not switch their attention away from the advancing group of four riders as they talked. Then they curtailed their exchange, as Crazy Pony signalled a change of pace. And the unshod mounts were cantered and then walked over a final two hundred yards: to be halted a hundred feet in front of the arc of wagons. The sub-chief held his lance as high as he could until the ponies were reined in. Then he lowered it and peered intently up at the area of wall above the gateway. While the braves with him made a blatant survey of the cannons which were aimed at them between the parked wagons.

'Major McCoy!' Crazy Pony yelled. 'I have message for big chief of fort!'

'The major ain't available, Crazy Pony!' Jack Floyd roared, cupping his big hands around his mouth to amplify his words. 'You talk to me!'

The sub-chief was about thirty. Five years or so older than the braves with him. All of them sparsely built but somehow strong-looking. Undernourished but displaying latent power in the set of their features and the fires in their dark eyes.

'That Jack Floyd?' Crazy Pony called, directing his powerful gaze towards the uniformed man who had spoken, and using a hand to shade his eyes from the sun.

'You got it!'

'Where McCoy?'

'A prisoner!'

The braves started to talk excitedly in their own language.

An order from the sub-chief silenced them, but their excitement remained high.

'For us, Jack Floyd? You know we come so you —'

'Not for you, Crazy Pony!' the sergeant cut in harshly.

Delight was replaced by suspicion on the thin faces of the braves. The sub-chief was as impassive as he had been from the start.

'I give you message from Chief Lone Horn, Jack Floyd! Chief will be most pleased it is to friend of Sioux I speak!'

'Somebody loves you, Jack!' Corporal Sibley bellowed across the compound from his position on the north wall. And produced a ripple of nervous laughter.

'Shut up, Leon!' Floyd snarled. And, in the same rancorous tone: 'Go ahead, Crazy Pony!'

'Lone Horn say Major McCoy and men from fort kill peaceful hunting party of our braves! Already we kill many horse soldiers and we burn lodges of many white eyes who steal Sioux land! Lone Horn and his warriors almost ready to lay down weapons and return to lodges! First must be given white eyes horse soldier Major McCoy!'

There was a short period of silence, then a mumbling of many exchanges: which were curtained when the sub-chief yelled:

'You hear me, Jack Floyd?'

'I hear you! But I figure you ain't through yet!'

Crazy Pony nodded. 'If you do not surrender him to us, we will attack! Many braves die! Perhaps Lone Horn! But fight will not end until every white eyes in fort dead! Horse soldiers and those who steal Sioux land! You give answer now, Jack Floyd!'

The sergeant with the iron-grey hair did not hesitate. 'Get the hell back to Lone Horn and tell him no deal!'

Many voices were raised within the fort: none of the words which were used reaching up to the centre of the south walkway so that they could be understood. But the tenor could be heard distinctly – anger that Floyd had not even considered the proposition.

Down below, out in front of the arc of wagons, Crazy Pony showed no inclination to offer the people in Fort Benedict a second chance. Just for part of a second his painted face showed a cruel smile to reveal his personal pleasure at Floyd's decision. Then he thrust the flag of truce high into the air again, spoke a one-word command and turned his mount with those of the braves to break into a gallop south.

By the time the thud of unshod hooves had faded from earshot, the bitter talk had petered out. But a wave of almost palpable resentment flooded through the warming air of morning towards the centre of the south walkway.

For stretched seconds, as he sensed himself the target of mass hatred, Floyd stood rigidly peering out towards the dust-enveloped bunch of riders. Then, with a snarl of rage, he whirled around.

'Shape up, you yellow-livered bastards! You're supposed to be soldiers! That's the uniform of the US Ninth Cavalry you're each wearin', Goddamnit! And that's a friggin' outfit that don't use a human life to bargain for an easy way out!'

'Shit on that, Jack, McCoy ain't hardly human!' Moody countered.

'Damn right!'

'I was for hangin' the sonofabitch in the first place!'

'We should've strung up Floyd first!'

'Just look at all of them redskins!'

'What the hell, it's too late now!'

'We're gonna have to put our lives on the line to save McCoy's stinkin' skin!'

At first, the embittered men allowed each other to voice individual feelings clearly. But as anger built, the shouts began to overlap and soon the noise was just an incoherent din.

Floyd allowed the men free rein on their emotions, his own feelings coming under control as he divided his attention between the enraged defenders of Benedict and the distant lines of Sioux. Perhaps aware of the danger that a trooper might do something more drastic than voice his anger, but accepting this as a calculated risk. Choosing to have the men with the fire of rage in their bellies rather than the cold of fear in their hearts. As, after a short exchange between Crazy Pony and Lone Horn, the Indian attack began.

110

They came slowly at first, walking their ponies as they checked over their weapons. Perhaps able to hear the barrage of voices from the fort. Until Lone Horn ordered a gallop, when the thunder of more than two hundred mounts at full stretch prevented any other sounds reaching their ears.

Floyd, sweat beads standing out on his forehead, drew the Army Colt from his holster and exploded a shot into the air. The shouting was abruptly curtailed and there was a part of a second of silence. Which was then invaded by the sound of the Sioux advance. And a few seconds later, as every man in a position to do so stared at the awesome scene to the south of the fort, the walkways seemed to tremble with the vibration of so many hooves pumping at the ground.

'Get to your post, mister,' Floyd growled, as he thrust the Colt back into its holster, dropped the field-glasses to the walkway and picked up his Springfield from where it rested against the top of the wall. 'And good luck.'

Steele shot a final glance southwards. To where more than just the mounted Sioux were on the move now. For the scattered cattle, spooked by the tremble of the ground beneath them, had begun to stampede ahead of the advance. While, in back of the galloping ponies – with riders who now started to vent high-pitched war whoops – smoke billowed and flames leapt. From the houses, barns and stables of homesteads which were subjected to a rain of flaming torches as the Indians swept around them.

Then he went fast down the ladder. There was no white terrier to greet him and follow him this time. For Dora Peachey had reclaimed her pet, to hold the dog close to her bosom throughout the long, tense night.

As the Virginian took long strides across the compound, he looked towards the barred window of the guardhouse. There were no faces in view anymore and he knew that the four officers and two troopers would now be in possession of the six carbines and six revolvers he ensured remained in the magazine after he issued selected civilians with weapons. The men still in the guardhouse, but poised to emerge when the time was right.

'The army needs more men like Jack Floyd!' Clem Burns

said with a catch in his throat and spraying more spittle down his chin.

'He's stupid!' Janet Manderson countered shrilly from behind the group of a dozen men armed with Springfields who were crowded into the area of the mess-hall doorway. 'Everyone hates McCoy! No one should have to die to protect him!'

'Hold your tongue, woman!' her husband snarled, taking a tighter grip on his carbine. 'You shame me!'

A deep-throated roar momentarily blanketed every other sound: as the cannon in the stable behind Gemma Sellers's house was fired. And even as eardrums continued to ring with the report, a cheer was raised by the men on the walkways. Which in turn was drowned by a second roar as another twelve-pound shot was exploded towards the Sioux.

Men shouted.

As, according to plan, the three artillery pieces behind the wagons were fired: to send shells arcing out above the heads of the troopers who lunged from the stable to race back to the fort.

A trooper – the thin, blond-haired Cass – scrambled down a ladder and doubled to the gates. To drag one of them wide so that the troopers manning the cannons could race into the cover of Benedict. He was the only man within the fort to move. Up on the walkways and in the towers the soldiers waited in frozen attitudes, carbines to the aim and fingers to the triggers. It was not possible to see the freed prisoners biding their time in the guardhouse. In the mess-hall, the civilians with guns looked at Steele. Some eagerly, others fearfully. Behind them, a few women sobbed. Jojo yapped.

Steele stood as if rooted to the ground, the Colt Hartford held two-handed across the base of his belly. He listened intently to the swelling volume of sound as the Sioux closed in. And peered with cracked eyes through the gate opened by Cass. Unable to see the Indians because of the half-circle of wagons.

Then, as the men who had tended the cannons raced for the opening, and the two Gatlings at the ends of the south wall crackled into vicious life, the Virginian snapped:

'Let's go!'

'But you were told to hold back until you were —' Boucher shouted.

Steele curled his lips away from his teeth to show a grin which looked as brutal as the chatter of rapid fire guns sounded.

'When there's killing to be done, feller,' he drawled, 'I'm not known for my reserve.'

Chapter Twelve

Carbine fire began to counterpoint the rapid staccato sound of the Gatling guns as Steele raced across the compound. This as the last man from outside spurted through the gateway and helped Cass to seal the opening and slide the fastening planks through their brackets.

Behind the Virginian, Tom Rosenberry, Stan Ivett and Manderson barged their way free of the crush in the mess-hall doorway and ran to the ladders serving the north, east and west walkways. Four more homesteaders gave chase. Which left five other men with rifles or carbines still inside.

Even before Steele reached the top of the ladder to the south-wall walkway, a half-dozen defenders had been hit. To stagger or be flung backwards, crumpling to the boarding or toppling to crash to the hard-packed dirt behind the buildings. Before turning to crouch behind the spiked top of the wall, Steele shot a grim-faced glance down and across the compound. He saw Clem Burns making for a ladder. And Gemma Sellers. Then George Peachey who was only a few years younger than Burns. None of these had been issued with guns. Clarke, the liquor drummer, had. And four homesteaders in their late thirties or early forties.

Jojo raced out of the doorway, nose to the ground and following the scent of Steele. Dora Peachey tried to plunge outside in the wake of her dog but was caught by Mrs Boucher and dragged tearfully back inside.

Steele went fast on all fours to squat beside Floyd as the sergeant reloaded his Springfield.

'We got friggin' big trouble, mister!' the sweating man gasped breathlessly. 'The bastards in the stable had four rounds to fire and they only blasted off two before they withdrew!'

He bobbed up, exploded a shot and ducked into cover to reload again. A moment later Steele rose and sent bullets in quick succession at the Sioux: as he made a fast survey of the scene outside the fort.

In the distance the flames and smoke continued to rise from the homesteads put to the torch. Closer, inert bodies and pony carcases and dismembered chunks of human and animal flesh showed where at least three of the artillery pieces had taken their toll of the attackers. Closer still, less shattered corpses, wounded braves, dead, injured and loose ponies revealed the accuracy of carbine and Gatling gun fire.

Much nearer to the fort the survivors of the initial assault – many more in number than those who were dead or wounded – circled the stockade at a full gallop. Controlling their ponies with knees and heels as they used both hands to fire rifles or release arrows. Fire arrows some of them, the flames making whooshing sounds in the slipstream before they thudded into the half-circle of wagons or into the stockade.

The whooping, shrieking, laughing braves circled twenty feet south of the Sellers place. But some had leapt clear of their mounts and dashed into the stable out back of the burning house. And now they could be seen, through breaks in the drifting smoke, as they manhandled the twelve-pounder into the doorway: to align the ugly barrel with the fort.

'They're crazy!' Floyd yelled, crouching down again under a hail of bullets and arrows after he had exploded another shot towards the Sioux. 'We're knockin' the bastards off like apples in a barrel yet they ain't regroupin'.'

'Listen, then look behind you, feller!' Steele shouted as he rose to pump two more shots from the Colt Hartford.

Five braves pitched from their horses, blood gushing from

115

body wounds, but it was not possible to know who scored hits.

'Oh, my God!' Floyd gasped as he witnessed the number of casualties the defenders had suffered.

Up on the walkways or sprawled below on the dirt. Many men screaming in fear and agony as waves of pain swept over them. More lying inertly in obvious death.

The uniformed hospital steward, a score of women and several civilian men were struggling to raise and carry the injured into shelter.

Troopers Adams and Helm and the fat Kupperman were among those uniformed men who did not move. Corporal Jordan, his youthful face curtained by blood, was among those who died as Floyd watched – lifted off his feet by a hail of bullets into his head and sent out of the tower and plunging to the ground.

'Listen to what?' the sergeant roared.

'The lousy Gatlings!' Steele bellowed back as he extracted spent shells and pushed fresh rounds into the Colt Hartford's acrid smelling chambers. 'You've lost them. They aren't firing! They always jam!'

'Shit!'

The cannon in the stable roared, the artillery piece set to the wrong elevation. It's shell smashed into the liquor salesman's wagon. One of many wagons set alight by fire arrows, pieces of the vehicle were hurled towards the gateway: adding their flames to those which were already eating at the stockade timbers on all sides of the fort.

'I got that bastard Lone Horn!' Sergeant Charlie Scott bellowed. 'I blasted the big friggin' chief, damnit!'

Then he screamed as an arrow burrowed its head into his ear. And drew himself up to his full height. Which left him exposed to arrows from two more bows and as many as six rifle shots. All hit him in the chest and drove him backward off the walkway. To smash down on the crouching form of Mrs Boucher. The woman had been trying to beat out the flames engulfing a trooper hit by a fire arrow. But suddenly her dress was alight as she was pitched across the trooper: struggled for a few seconds but was unable to get out from under the dead weight of Scott.

116

Fires burned in other areas of the fort, started by flaming arrows which whooshed in over the walls: many to land harmlessly and go out on the compound, but others finding fuel in the walls and roofs of the post buildings.

A second twelve-pounder shell exploded from Gemma Sellers's stable. And this time the brave who aimed the cannon found his target. Both gates were ripped off their hinges and scattered across the compound in lethal fragments of flying wood.

The gross Mrs Rosenberry was a victim of this, a massive piece of splintered timber spinning forcefully into her bulging belly and almost cutting her in half. This as she went across the compound at a waddling run, brandishing a carbine taken from a dead trooper.

Steele and Floyd were at the south east tower by then, struggling to unjam the Gatling which had gone out of action just before Corporal Jordan was hit.

Bullets and arrows continued to lash at the fort and soldiers and civilians kept up a counter barrage. But Indians and whites alike were now firing blind. Through billowing black smoke from raging fires on the walls, in the buildings and aboard the wagons. Smoke that stung the eyes and seared the throat with the acrid taint of burnt gunpowder which it carried.

With nothing to aim at, both men concentrated on emptying the hopper of the Gatling to find where the cartridges were blocking entry to the breech.

'I never seen Indians this crazy!' Floyd yelled. 'I've fought Apaches, Comanches, Kiowa and the Sioux before! But they never thrown everythin' into one attack! I figured that sneaky bastard Lone Horn to be smarter than this! There! Freed the stinkin' gun!'

The sweating man withdrew his hands from the hopper, his fingers red-raw and blistered from clawing at hot metal.

'I'll load!' he shouted. 'Oh, Jesus!'

The reason for his blasphemy was the actions of a group of braves close to the fort. A half dozen of them had lunged from their ponies and run to the blazing wagon immediately opposite the shattered gateway of the post. And were now risking severe burns as they hauled and pushed to move the blazing vehicle off the trail.

One, then a second brave was pitched to the ground by bullets blasted out through the gateway.

'Fire, fire, fire!' Floyd shrieked.

Steele swung the Gatling on its mounting and began to crank the handle of the ten-barrel gun. And saw three more braves go down, blood gushing from body and head wounds.

But the defensive half-circle of wagons had been breached by then. And moments later the grinning Crazy Pony and another sub-chief led war whooping braves at a flat-out gallop through the billowing smoke that was all that stood between them and entry to Fort Benedict.

They rode in a column of two, firing wildly. And the front runners escaped the deadly hail of bullets from the Gatling, for the hopper was empty. But then, for perhaps fifteen seconds, Jack Floyd fed cartridges and Steele cranked the handle. The sergeant laughing hysterically and the Virginian's face wearing a fixed killer's grin. As spent shellcases piled around their feet and screaming Sioux braves pitched from ponies: the writhing wounded piled with the inert dead in the smoke-veiled gap left by the movement of the wagon.

Then, as the following braves had to jump their mounts over the human barrier, the rapid-fire gun became jammed again.

'Come on, keep friggin' firin'!' Floyd snarled, as he hurled more shells into the hopper and became aware that the gun was silent.

But Steele had already whirled away from the Gatling, to snatch up the Colt Hartford. And it was the rifle that cracked out. Once, twice and then again. The Virginian aiming down into the compound now, his brutal grin broadening as he experienced a keener sense of achievement: seeing individual braves sent sprawling to the ground as a result of his carefully placed shots.

'The hell with you, mister!' Floyd snarled, and made to get behind the Gatling.

But Crazy Pony, as unaware as the sergeant that the rapid-fire gun was out of action again, realised the Gatling was the major threat to the success of the Sioux attack. And, from the cover of the gallows platform, he fired three shells in quick succession from his Winchester. The first hit the hopper and ricocheted harmlessly out over the wall. But the second took Floyd in the shoulder and half turned him: and the third tunnelled in through his forehead and burst out of the top of his skull.

Floyd died with his too-short lips formed into a curse he never had the time to voice. And was tipped out of the tower to plummet, limbs trailing limply, to the dirt outside the fort.

Steele, unaffected by the death of Jack Floyd, sent a shot towards the gallows platform and then went at a crouched run along the east wall walkway. Having to go around or climb over the slumped form of dead and wounded troopers. One of the injured was Sergeant Dave Durrell, who lay on his back, his lips moving in a silent prayer as blood oozed up through the fingers of both hands which were interlocked around an arrow embedded in the centre of his belly.

Veiled by smoke which coiled and billowed up from the burning officers' quarters, Steele climbed halfway down the ladder in the north-west corner of the fort and jumped the rest of the way. One of his booted feet smashed into the face of the grey-haired Lieutenant Dunbar. But the officer was beyond the reach of mortal pain for two arrows were sunk deep into his chest, left of centre.

Steele squatted down against the rear of the major's house to eject the four spent shell cases from the rifle's chambers and reload. As the final round was pushed home by his gloved thumb, Jojo lunged joyfully at him: standing on his hind legs to lick the Virginian's bristled and sweat-run cheek.

'Atta boy,' Steele murmured, and spared a moment to ruffle the fur at the terrier's neck before he stood up.

Just as a brave with blood on his face lunged out of the smoke.

Steele triggered a shot across a range of six feet and the bullet tunnelled completely through the Indian's torso, the power of its upward trajectory acting to raise the brave on tiptoes before flipping him over on to his back.

Jojo growled, snarled and barked. And Steele whirled as a man screamed in pain. It was one of the sub-chiefs, his war bonnet gone and his hair charred by flames. He had a toma-hawk raised with the intention of hurling it at the Virginian. But abruptly there was a new target: the white terrier who had sunk his teeth into the sub-chief's thigh just above the right knee. And hung there, tail flapping and extended claws inflicting lesser damage on the Indian's leg.

Steele was in a half-crouch, the split seam in his right pants leg gaping. Faster than he could have cocked, aimed and fired the Colt Hartford, he drew the knife and sent it spinning across twelve feet of smoke-filled air to thud the blade deep into the Indian's chest.

The sub-chief vented a deep-throated roar of agony and released the tomahawk a moment before the vicious blade would have severed the body of the small dog. The terrier clung tenaciously to the flesh of the Indian even after it was dead and the corpse was sprawled on the ground.

'Here, Jojo!' Steele snapped, and a trace of humour entered his killer's grin as the dog obeyed, tongue hanging out between blood-stained teeth. 'Raw meat'll make you vicious.'

A man shouted: 'Fire!' In a voice that was firm and calm. Then again: 'Fire!' Two seconds later: 'Fire!'

Steele recognised the voice as that of Major McCoy. Coming from the other side of the row of burning buildings under the north wall of the fort. Each of the major's commands answered by a fusillade of shots which sounded as one.

The Virginian pulled the knife from the dead sub-chief's chest, wiped the blade on his own pants leg and replaced it in the boot sheath. Then taking advantage of as-yet-unburnt timber walls and the less reliable cover of constantly moving clouds of smoke, he made his way to and along the gap be-tween the commanding officer's house and the command office.

Out in front of the blazing buildings, too close to the flames for comfort, but gaining the occasional temporary cover of the drifting smoke, McCoy was in command of thirty or more survivors. A line of officers, troopers and civilian men and women. Each alternate man or woman in the line dropping into a crouch to reload his or her carbine while the rest trig-gered shots across the compound on McCoy's command.

Colvard was there. And the pot-bellied Captain Starling. The tall and fat Trooper Williams, the almost chinless Girling and the two men who had shared the guardhouse cell with the officers. Stan and Iris Ivett, Manderson, Clem Burns, the bespectacled Clarke and Gemma Sellers.

Janet Manderson was dead, as was George Peachey. Four more civilians Steele did not know by name. And a half dozen troopers. As many were wounded, soldiers and civilians alike. The corpses and the pain-wracked bodies of the injured lay still or writhed where they had fallen: the gaps they left in the line ignored by those who survived. All hate-filled attention directed towards the gateless entrance to Fort Benedict. Through which Sioux braves continued to gallop their ponies. On to a compound littered with their own and white dead and injured: their unfeeling or already punished flesh trampled by the ponies of the Indians, the horses which had escaped from the burning stable of the fort and two steers which had been somehow caught up in the frenzied attack.

McCoy, with his sabre in one hand and an Army Colt in the other, took careful aim with the revolver and skilfully picked off braves who escaped the hail of bullets directed at the gateway.

Other men, with carbines or revolvers, acted as sharpshooters in a similar fashion: from the cover of the cookhouse and the barrack which was not yet totally engulfed by flames.

Then, suddenly, as Steele moved into the gap left by George Peachey and exploded a shot in isolation towards the gateway, the inpouring of braves was curtailed.

A break appeared in the smoke from the blazing wagons and those in direct line with the gateway were able to see, under or over the gallows platform, out to what lay beyond the gap in the half-circle of vehicles.

Chief Lone Horn was out there, bloody from Charlie Scott's bullet, but able to sit his pony: supported by the two sub-chiefs who flanked him. The trio at the front of a group of more than a hundred braves.

'Hold your fire!' McCoy ordered. Aware that if he could see out of Benedict, the Sioux chief could see into the fort.

And what Lone Horn and his warriors could see, at longer

range than those in the post, were the massed dead and dying, and the orderly line of surviving defenders. Closer to the Indians were the sprawled corpses and groaning wounded who had been blasted off their ponies far short of their objective.

Smoke billowed to veil the opposing combatants from each other.

'Ready and aim!' McCoy snapped, against the crackle of flames and the sharper sounds of splitting timber.

A howl, as from an animal in distress, punctuated the white man's order. But from beyond the walls of the fort.

Weapons – rifles, bows, knives, revolvers and tomahawks – were hurled out of cover on to the compound. With gasps of alarm, the defenders swung their carbines towards the sounds. Then took aim at the braves who stepped into sight. Indians with defiant expressions but clutching their hands to their heads in a sign of surrender.

'Hold fire!' McCoy yelled, less composed as he recognised the danger that revenge bent men and women might gun down the unarmed and defeated Sioux. An action which would certainly bring the massed braves pouring into the fort.

No one fired.

The flames raged.

'Go!' McCoy shouted.

One brave took a tentative step towards the gateway. The others followed his example. All turned their backs on the aimed carbines but kept their hands on their heads until they were lost to sight in the smoke. Fourteen Sioux braves had been inside the fort unscathed. Ten more crawled or staggered out, dripping blood to mark their back trails.

'Advance!' McCoy commanded.

The troopers and officers complied at once but the civilians were quick to follow: suggesting this was how it had been when the major first mounted the rearguard action against the attack. The line, with McCoy at the centre, advanced slowly across the compound, stepping over the dead and ignoring the cries of the wounded: dividing for a few moments to get around the obstacle of the gallows. Some men emerged from the flanking buildings to fall in at either end.

Grim-faced, smoke- and sweat-stained, some with blood on

their faces and clothing, they all came to a halt on McCoy's order at the fort entrance. Then, as the major went on ahead, towards the gap in the half-circle of wagons, the line broke to form a group: so that all could look through the gate to where the commanding officer of Fort Benedict moved into the smoke.

Steele elected to climb the ladder to the south-west tower. Jojo waited patiently at the foot.

The main group of Sioux braves still sat their ponies in back of Lone Horn and the two sub-chiefs. Waiting for the braves from the fort to join them.

The smoke diminished, but the stench of burning remained as strong as ever in the hot air of morning.

Some of the braves on foot captured loose ponies and swung astride them. The injured were helped up to sit behind the riders.

For long moments, as the last of the smoke from the charred wagons disappeared and McCoy could be seen standing in isolation out front of the fort, the dejection of the Indians was displaced by angry tension. But then, at a word from Lone Horn, the sub-chiefs turned his and their own ponies around. The main body of Indians divided into two so that their injured leader could be escorted among them. Then the whole bunch rode slowly south: towards the ridge over which they had first shown themselves.

McCoy holstered his Colt and slid the sabre back into its scabbard. Then swung around, grimly triumphant. 'Attend to the wounded!' he snapped. 'Battle's over!'

Carbines and revolvers were dropped to the ground and men and women dashed in every direction: civilians to search for dead and wounded husbands, wives or friends while the soldiers tended to whichever blood-stained uniformed man was closest to them.

Dora Peachey rushed to reclaim the whining Jojo before she went to the spot where her husband lay crumpled in death.

'Captain Starling, detail fire-fighting squads! Lieutenant Colvard, get me casualty figures!'

McCoy barked the orders as he strode in through the gate-less entrance of Benedict.

'Don't, Leon!' This from the red-haired, squint-eyed Trooper Hardy, his voice ringing out from the broken windows of the barrack.

'I'm with you, Leon!' Arnie Moody yelled. And emerged from the cookhouse as Sibley stepped on to the threshold of the barrack. 'We lost too many good buddies to save the friggin' major!'

Four shots rang out. But those from the Springfields of Sibley and Moody fired the bullets down into the ground on which they fell, dying with grimaces of naked hatred on their faces and blood spilling from their chests.

For the Colt Hartford aimed at the corporal and the Army Colt of Colvard swung towards Moody were the first of the quartet of guns to be fired.

Tension was abruptly high again, seeming to crackle louder than the flames. As faces, tear- and sweat-run, gaunt with shock, contorted by pain or heavy with grief swung towards the areas of fresh violence.

'Dear God, no more!' Edward Boucher wailed from where he was down on his knees, hands pressed together in an attitude of prayer.

Gemma Sellers blew out a stream of smoke from a freshly lit cigar. 'Arnie will like it better he was shot instead of hung,' she said flatly.

McCoy's composure was ruffled for just a second. Then, after the two comments, he nodded his thanks to the lieutenant and watched with curiosity as Steele came down the ladder. As did everyone else. The Ivetts, the dull-faced Manderson, Dora Peachey holding her pet dog; Williams, Cass and Girling; Clarke and Clem Burns; Starling and Colvard. Other survivors – military and civilian – the Virginian knew by sight but had no names for.

'Lieutenant Colvard had a duty to perform, sir,' the major said as Steele ambled out on to the compound, picking his way between the wounded and the dead and the uninjured. 'But you . . .'

'Considered that Sergeant Floyd enlisted me, major,' Steele answered. 'And if a man joins any group, he has to abide by the rules. Long as I'm in the army, I have to reckon that one good soldier is worth more than two bad ones.'

He shot a rueful glance towards the charred remains of the mess hall from which wisps of smoke continued to rise. His gear had been in there. But at least the stable out back of the destroyed Sellers's house was still in one piece. The Sioux should have had no reason to slaughter his black stallion.

'I thank you,' McCoy said gruffly.

'You're welcome . . . ' He crossed over the threshold of the gateless fort and added: ' . . . feller.'

If the retreating Sioux heard the burst of gunfire, they did not even look back at Benedict.

McCoy nodded curtly, worked the expression of grim triumph on to his round and weathered face again, and strode in his martinet gait across the no-longer-spick-and-span compound. As the tending of the wounded recommenced.

'The hostiles could simply be withdrawing to regroup, Mr Steele,' Colvard said.

'Not for a long time, I reckon,' the Virginian answered. 'Lone Horn knows Jack Floyd's dead but he saw the major out there, large as life.'

Colvard nodded. 'Like to add my thanks, sir. When we were in a tight spot, he showed he doesn't ride his men hard for nothing.'

'Lieutenant!' McCoy roared. 'I gave you an order!'

Colvard looked regretfully at Steele and the open country beyond him: almost as if he envied the civilian his freedom to leave the ravaged fort and its ruin- and corpse-littered surroundings. He sighed.

'Just wish he hadn't massacred that hunting party to start all this.'

'He said himself that he allows a man the one mistake.'

'Mr Colvard!' McCoy bellowed.

'Goodbye, sir.'

'Sure, feller,' the Virginian said softly, and touched the brim of his hat . . . 'DISMISS.'*

---

* From this book. You are invited to fall in for the next story in the Adama Steele series.

ADAM STEELE:
THE VIOLENT PEACE
by George G. Gilman

In this fast-moving story of high adventure and daring,
Adam Steele sets out on a mission with a deadly purpose.
A vendetta that will turn old friends into enemies, and
bring a slow or sudden death to the marked men.

Abraham Lincoln is assassinated whilst at the theatre in
Washington. A great and honourable president is mourned
by many, but his passing brings rejoicing to those
Southerners defeated in the Civil War. Meanwhile Adam
Steele finds he has a private grief to mourn, when he
discovers the body of his father slowly swinging on a
makeshift gallows. This is a sorrow he cannot share with
other men. He is determined to have his revenge and sets
out on a trail of blood and violence.

On sale at newsagents and booksellers everywhere.

NEW ENGLISH LIBRARY

ADAM STEELE:
VALLEY OF BLOOD
by George G. Gilman

An action-packed western featuring Adam Steele In a tale
of blood and revenge. In the fourth volume of this new
western series from George G. Gilman, the author of the
best-selling EDGE, Steele comes face to face with a man he
can only hate and despise, a man whose insatiable greed
leads him to terrorise the lives of innocent people. Only
Steele's split second timing and his cold nerve make death
pass him by, and achieve his aim – to destroy Chance.

On sale at booksellers and newsagents everywhere.

NEW ENGLISH LIBRARY

NEL BESTSELLERS

T046 133	HOW GREEN WAS MY VALLEY	*Richard Llewellyn*	£1.00
T039 560	I BOUGHT A MOUNTAIN	*Thomas Firbank*	95p
T033 988	IN THE TEETH OF THE EVIDENCE	*Dorothy L. Sayers*	90p
T038 149	THE CARPET BAGGERS	*Harold Robbins*	£1.50
T040 917	TO SIR WITH LOVE	*E. R. Braithwaite*	75p
T041 719	HOW TO LIVE WITH A NEUROTIC DOG	*Stephen Baker*	75p
T040 925	THE PRIZE	*Irving Wallace*	£1.65
T034 755	THE CITADEL	*A. J. Cronin*	£1.10
T042 189	STRANGER IN A STRANGE LAND	*Robert Heinlein*	£1.25
T037 053	79 PARK AVENUE	*Harold Robbins*	£1.25
T042 308	DUNE	*Frank Herbert*	£1.50
T045 137	THE MOON IS A HARSH MISTRESS	*Robert Heinlein*	£1.25
T040 933	THE SEVEN MINUTES	*Irving Wallace*	£1.50
T038 130	THE INHERITORS	*Harold Robbins*	£1.25
T035 689	RICH MAN, POOR MAN	*Irwin Shaw*	£1.50
T037 134	EDGE 27: DEATH DRIVE	*George G. Gilman*	75p
T037 541	DEVIL'S GUARD	*Robert Elford*	£1.25
T042 774	THE RATS	*James Herbert*	80p
T042 340	CARRIE	*Stephen King*	80p
T042 782	THE FOG	*James Herbert*	90p
T033 740	THE MIXED BLESSING	*Helen Van Slyke*	£1.25
T037 061	BLOOD AND MONEY	*Thomas Thompson*	£1.50
T038 629	THIN AIR	*Simpson & Burger*	95p
T038 602	THE APOCALYPSE	*Jeffrey Konvitz*	95p

NEL P.O. BOX 11, FALMOUTH TR10 9EN, CORNWALL

Postage charge:

U.K. Customers. Please allow 25p for the first book plus 10p per copy for each additional book ordered to a maximum charge of £1.05 to cover the cost of postage and packing, in addition to cover price.

B.F.P.O. & Eire. Please allow 25p for the first book plus 10p per copy for the next 8 books, thereafter 5p per book, in addition to cover price.

Overseas Customers. Please allow 40p for the first book plus 12p per copy for each additional book, in addition to cover price.

Please send cheque or postal order (no currency).

Name ....

Address ....

....

Title ....

While every effort is made to keep prices steady, it is sometimes necessary to increase prices at short notice. New English Library reserve the right to show on covers and charge new retail prices which may differ from those advertised in the text or elsewhere.